The Bonnie Neuk Tea Room
Paranormal Mystery Series

THE BONNIE NEUK TEA ROOM:

FRIENDS AND UNINVITED
~~GUESTS~~ *Ghosts*

By
Connie Hope

SPIDER BOOKS
PUBLISHING

The Bonnie Neuk Tea Room:
Friends and Uninvited Guests/Ghosts

Copyright @ 2014 Connie Hope and Cooking by Connie, LLC

All rights reserved. Published by: Cooking by Connie LLC
and Spider Book Publishing, Fort Myers, Florida.

No part of this book may be used or reproduced by any means, graphic, electronic, or mechanical, including photocopying, recording, taping or by any information storage retrieval system without the written permission of the publisher except in the case of brief quotations embodied in critical articles and reviews. For information regarding permission, write to Spider Books Publishing, Attention Permissions, 2968 Ribbon Ct, Ft Myers, FL 33905

LCCN: 2014947055

ISBN-10: 099165384X

ISBN-13: 978-0-9916538-4-3

Written and created by Connie Hope
Cover by John Hope

Cover illustration by Kayla Perales

Cover & Interior designed by
Jennifer FitzGerald / Mother Spider Publishing
http://www.motherspider.com

Edited by Virginia Schuler

www.thebonnieneuktearoom.com
thebonnieneuktearoom@gmail.com

In loving memory of my Grandmother,

Daisy Hamilton Pyatt Campbell Thornall,

who owned and operated

"The Bonnie Neuk Tea Room"

in Metuchen, New Jersey in 1932.

You are my inspiration and my

guide.

TABLE OF CONTENTS

Thanks to people who gave me insight to help me write this book.

The Bonnie Neuk Tea Room: Friends and Uninvited ~~Guest~~ Ghosts

I have always read the acknowledgment pages of books, because I know that sometimes these people have played a vital role in the undertaking of its writing. For those who have never tried to put a book together, it is a monumental task. I have learned that each step of the way, which is why I need to thank so many.

Thank you to many people in Metuchen. the zoning officer Chris Cosenza for walking me through the process of obtaining zoning for construction of my tea room in Metuchen. He really put a light on the process. Tom Falcetto, in the County Health Department, who helped with the number of bathrooms and the health requirements for the Bonnie Neuk.

And the two secretaries at the township building in Metuchen Borough, Sharon and Jill, helped get messages and gave me suggestions for workings in the Borough. The Metuchen Chamber of Commerce were very informative and helpful throughout the process.

Ginny Schuler who proofread the pages as I wrote them. What a dear friend to encourage the starting of this novel, and she is the reason I have finished. She told me she was hooked. Wow, how could I not finish the book.

I used my own Vermont Teddy Bear to have an artist's rendition of him for my book cover. I love my bear.

Denise Curcio, for being my sounding board when I needed one. ...from menu plans to house plans to ghost visiting to holistic things in the book. She and I are spiritual friends who during the years have shared many out-of-the-ordinary experiences. We have gone to many mediums together.

The New Jersey State Police Historian Division confirming the dates there was a Metuchen Police Barrack at my grandmother's house (1927-1932). The barrack was closed in 1932 because of finances and the Depression. Shortly after that my grandmother opened her tea room.

Bobbie Schwartz, who owns the Wisteria Tea Room and Café in Ft Myers, Florida She not only helped me with my menu, but she also showed me her kitchen and let me pick her brain for ideas.

In 2013, Critique Critter group was formed from my writing club, Gulf Coast Writers Association. We had four members. I want to say a special THANK YOU for reading and critiquing each chapter.

Deborah Keleman, who taught me to read tea leaves and tarot cards, at the Labyrinth in Fort Myers, Florida. It was a fun and interesting evening. Thanks.

A special thanks to my dad, who if he hadn't put the information in his genealogy book about my grandmother's tea room, I never would have known about it and this book would not have been written. I know you have guided me along my road to writing.

I have dedicated this book to my grandmother, for without her tenacity and forthrightness, again, I would not have written this book.

THE BONNIE NEUK TEA ROOM:
FRIENDS AND UNINVITED ~~GUESTS~~ *Ghosts*

CHAPTER 1

"A true warrior, like tea, shows their strength in hot water"
Ancient Chinese proverb

Victoria's phone rang, interrupting her meeting with her divorce attorney. An unfamiliar voice asked, ***"Why don't you open a tea room in Metuchen like your grandmother had many years ago."***

Immediately, the line went dead. *Did my grandmother really have a tea room? When and where? And who just called me?* She checked her phone for a number, but none appeared.

Attorney Rhonda Miller had been speaking, but Victoria hadn't heard a word. "Victoria, are you with me?" asked Rhonda. "You look as if you're a million miles away and have seen a ghost."

"I guess I wasn't here, and I'm not sure where I am.

1

Sorry," apologized Victoria. "So much has changed in the last year. Both my parents died within eleven months of each other. I was close to both of them." What had my mother said? "If you find a penny, know that I am thinking of you and love you. If you're at a crossroad and the penny's head is up, it is a positive sign about what you are doing. If the head is down, you might want to rethink it or keep trying."

Victoria has found many pennies in the last few months. Her mother was supporting and loving her even in death. *Thanks, Mom!*

"Since separating from my husband of twenty-five years and getting a divorce, everything seems so final, so unreal. I guess I'm a little shell shocked. Do you hear voices when you're shell shocked?"

Rhonda smiled. "I don't think so, but who knows?" and passed it off as an amusing verbal exchange.

Victoria squirmed in the large chair and tried to absorb all that had happened in the last few weeks, ending in a short court appearance to finalize her divorce. She and Tony had separated six months ago after Victoria caught him with another woman. She wanted out—out of their marriage and out of their beautiful house. On her own was the order of the day.

Things always happen for a reason. The reason is not always immediately apparent but in time reveals itself. She had packed her things—her mother's things, her grandmother's things. As an only child, all their possessions belonged to her now. Box after box of "stuff" packed away. She had moved out of the house and into a small rental apartment within two weeks of the incident, putting everything in storage except for her favorite stuffed bear.

Mr. Ted Bear was a two-foot bear her grandmother Thorn had given her as a toddler. It had gone everywhere with her. He was her comfort bear. She needed him with

her. Now more than ever.

She and Tony had three wonderful children who were grown and on their own, progressing diligently with their lives. Each had gone in a different direction, but one that was right for each of them.

One learns with difficulty how to parent. You take on all the responsibility to shelter, nurture, protect, and supervise their homework. Day after day, hour by hour, we are involved in their lives. Then suddenly, we're supposed to stop! The child is now an adult and no longer lives at home. It's challenging to bite one's tongue and not ask, "When was the last time you ate something?" It's no longer the mother's place. The role has changed from mother-protector to mother-friend. Not bad, just different. It is a struggle to give up all the overseeing that comes with parenting. It's something we learn and re-learn. Fortunately, our children are more than happy to help teach us. In this case, with the children not living in the house, it was easier to change.

The house Victoria and her husband built was situated on Tony's father's land. All their money had gone into building it, but the title had never been put in both names. However, because she and Tony had been together for more than twenty-five years, her attorney felt she could ask for a sizable settlement. He and his family were well off, and Rhonda believed the additional effort would be worth it in the end. The results of the court hearing would be known in a few days.

The hurt was new and continued to sting. When you love someone and he betrays you, it's difficult to trust again. But Victoria knew she had to move on and not look back.

Having worked as an office manager for a small business firm for several years, Victoria had experience in personnel, bookkeeping, and marketing. She was good at it and made a decent salary, but wanted a different focus—something that would utilize her creativity to the fullest. This was to be her new life, and she anticipated it with a passion.

Thoughts of making jellies and jams to sell in local markets and stores, maybe even churches and bazaars, came to mind. Or painting, taking photos, sewing curtains, or writing…pursuing something creative, perhaps even spiritual. She was spiritual and wanted to explore new opportunities. She could invest the settlement money wisely and live off the proceeds, but what would she do with her time. She wanted a labor of love, not of money. First on her list was a course in Reiki, a technique for stress reduction and relaxation that produces spiritual healing. It is administered by "laying on hands." The life force energy is channeled through the practitioner to the recipient. This would explore her spiritual side. Next, take a mediumship course held in Lily Dale, New York— communicating with the dead could be eye opening. She always wanted to learn to read tea leaves and tarot cards. Another avenue to explore. This would be a good beginning, but she needed a passion to work toward. Lots of options lay ahead.

Sitting on the newly acquired sofa in her living room, Victoria was reading the local Blue Bell, Pennsylvania newspaper and sipping a cup of Darjeeling tea. Darjeeling has been called the "champagne of tea" and is grown solely in the Darjeeling region of West Bengal, India. The first sip is sweet, dry, and fruity. But it seems to impart a unique lift of additional flavor at the end of your sip. Inhaling it was divine. Her short, blond hair had been freshly washed and wrapped in a bath towel. The newspaper featured an article on antiques and their declining value in today's world, as well as an announcement about a new tea room opening in the next town. It described the increasing popularity of tea. People were changing from coffee or cappuccino to all types of teas. Tea rooms were popping up all over the country. She said out loud, "I have always loved tea." Abruptly, Victoria's cell phone rang and startled her.

"Hi, Victoria. It's Rhonda Miller." There was a moment of complete silence. "We got the determination on your divorce settlement! Are you sitting down?"

"Yes. Did we do okay?" she asked.

"Better than okay. We did great! Tony wanted things settled quickly. I negotiated you an initial payment of $800,000, plus $500 a week for ten years."

Victoria was overwhelmed as she tried to absorb the figures.

"Stop trying to calculate it in your head. It's $26,000 a year for ten years and the initial settlement of $800,000, which totals $1,060,000. Congratulations." Rhonda's voice revealed a tone of self satisfaction. "So, what are you planning to do with the rest of your life?"

"Thank you so much, Rhonda. It was your determination and hard work that made the difference. What **am** I going to do?"

Moments later, Victoria remembered the voice on the cell phone. *Maybe I could open a tea room in Metuchen, the town where my grandmother may have started her venture.* My grandmother was my touchstone in life. We had a special bond despite the fact I was in my teens when she left this earth plane. Could a tea room do well in this day and age? Coffee was very popular. Could I make the tea room a success and make money? I need to research tea rooms, their situation in today's economy as well as check out other small business ventures. Lots of things to check into and consider. Where to find information? Of course, the Internet! Time to purchase a laptop computer and a new cell phone. I'd like to be able to do

some texting, but I'll stick with the "dumb phone" right now, rather than those new smart ones. Communication is essential. Learning new things takes time and patience.

She was about to emerge as a different Victoria Storm. Standing five feet, eight inches tall, with short blond hair and blue eyes, she had stepped into the mirror of Alice and emerged with the grand prize—her freedom, a considerable amount of money, and a brand new life. She needed to make the most from this situation.

CHAPTER 2

"My dear, if you could give me a cup of tea
to clear my muddle of a head, I should better
understand your affairs."
Charles Dickens

I spent the next few weeks researching various ventures. Maybe relocate to Florida, or open a dress shop? Why would I go to Florida? What do I know about retail stores? Or that constant, recurring thought, perhaps open a tea room. What do I know about tea rooms? I did a little searching on the Web and became somewhat intrigued. Time to make an appointment with my favorite psychic, Maria Pole.

I called Maria and left a message. Within minutes she returned my call, and we made an appointment for the next afternoon. I remember previous discussions where she had hinted about changes occurring in my marriage. Changes... that was an understatement. This would be an interesting session.

On a whim, I returned to my old hometown of Metuchen, New Jersey, using the opportunity to look around, visit my parents' and families' graves, and maybe drop-in on two friends I kept in touch with in the "Brainy Borough," as Metuchen was called. It would be fun to touch base with my high school friends, Laine and Raphael, and Aunt Jeannie, who was a close friend and neighbor of my mother. Driving through town, I experienced a feeling of calm, something that has eluded me for some time. Maybe this would be a nice place to regroup and start anew. Metuchen was a small town where everyone looked out for one another. It had a Main Street, not a feature of many towns today. My childhood and teenage years in Metuchen were a memorable experience.

My first stop was the First Presbyterian Church cemetery to place flowers on my parents' grave. I always felt at peace there. I knew they weren't in that ground; their souls were in the light, but it was comforting to be there. We had large family plots located in two areas. My grandfather, who I never knew, and my grandma, Daisy Thorn, were buried there. Also my great-grandparents and my great uncle, Les Thorn. Alongside my mother and father was my Uncle Will. He was killed tragically in a bus and train accident on January 8, 1944, my grandmother's birthday, only days before shipping overseas as an Army sergeant to defend his country. Placing flowers on the graves, I had a strange feeling I was not alone. I turned my head to both sides, but encountered nothing but a strong gust of wind. Hm..m

On the way back to the car, my cell phone rang. *"If you check out your father's book, you'll learn some new and interesting things,"* the speaker informed me.

"What things?" I said, but the phone had gone dead.

"Hello, hello." No one answered. "Well, that seems weird. How does this person know that my father wrote a book let alone what's in it?" This is very troubling. How did they get my phone number? No data was listed on my phone.

I drove around town observing the stores, banks, and restaurants lining Main Street, and picked up a copy of the *Metuchen Recorder*. I checked out the library in hopes of locating my dad's book that the mysterious phone caller had suggested. If there was time, I'd stop to see my old friends. I parked, left my purse under the seat of the car, grabbed my notepad and pen, and walked in approaching the front desk.

"Good afternoon." The sign on the desk read Elizabeth Harp, Librarian. "I'm looking for a book on Metuchen's genealogy by my father, John Thorn. I think it might be in the historical or genealogy section or maybe even the archives." I looked around at the many changes to the library. "It's been a long time since I've been here."

"Well, we've unquestionably undergone major improvements," Elizabeth informed me. "Our reference librarian, Tammy O'Reilly, can easily direct you to the correct location. If it's not in the catalog, we'll check out the old archives section downstairs."

She motioned to Tammy, who indicated with a hand wave that I should follow her over to the card catalog. We checked but it was not listed. "The archives are in a remote section of the basement. A bit spooky. Follow me and we'll go hunting."

"My father wrote this book about the town and our family and donated copies to the library many years ago. You may not even have it anymore."

"Your father wrote a book? That's cool. Let's check out the historical reference section in the back. These books are rarely used."

We searched all the shelves for the book. Nothing.

"I'm sure he donated a copy," I said.

"Let's try in several smaller rooms." Again, nothing. "We might find it in the far closet." The air smelled musty and stale. Ahead was a large closet with many shelves crammed full of dusty books. Tammy and I scanned the shelves. There didn't seem to be any order, but on the bottom shelf, there it was by John Thorn—*The Farmers of Metuchen*. Kneeling down to retrieve it, I experienced an unexpected surge of pride.

"Well, we did have one, but a bit of dust comes with it," Tammy laughed as she dusted it off.

"May I take the book upstairs and look through it?"

"Yes, of course," said Tammy.

I found a comfortable chair and sat down. Since the book was considered a reference volume, it could not be checked out. Skimming over the pages for almost an hour, I came across a small excerpt from *The Metuchen Recorder* about my grandmother's tea room.

It was headlined:

"State Police Station is Tea Room in Metuchen Borough"

Mrs. Daisy Thorn, who is well known in Metuchen and vicinity, is pleased to announce the opening of a tea room at her home on Middlesex Avenue, the former headquarters of the New Jersey State Police.

A delicious luncheon for fifty cents will be featured every day, while a special Sunday evening supper will be offered at the small cost of forty cents per person. Home cooking will be the password at the "Bonnie Neuk," located at 913 Middlesex Avenue. While a genuine and sincere effort to please is expected to be the basis upon which a satisfied and ever increasing patronage will be built, a special room is being reserved for organizations or groups wishing to play cards and drink flavored teas as a "topping off" feature of their dinner.

This was exciting, definite proof that my grandmother did own and operate a tea room. Although no date was given as to the opening, I'm assuming it was somewhere between 1930 and 1935. I could check further with the New Jersey State Police to learn when their Metuchen headquarters had closed and the tea room opened.

While using the library's computers, I Googled "tea rooms in the early twentieth century." I discovered that the American tea room is intertwined with three events occurring early in the century. The growing practice of motoring by automobile to rural areas outside of cities was becoming popular. The movement to prohibit alcohol brought significant changes to social events. And women's role in American society was evolving. In earlier centuries, women dressed in long, restrictive clothing, had no vote, could not hold public office, and rarely ventured outside the home. The tea room eventually became their threshold to independence. Women not only wanted to earn a living, but also wished to be independent and to mingle with others from various walks of life. Some dreamed of owning a business as a means of expressing their creativity and self expression. My grandmother was a forerunner in the new women's movement. In some ways she was ahead of her time. What a hoot! My grandmother was a great entrepreneur and role model for me. Unexpectedly, there in the corner by the bookshelves was a penny—heads up.

My grandmother's tea room was called the Bonnie Neuk. What an unusual name. Her name was Daisy—why would she call it the Bonnie Neuk? I went on the Internet to check out what "Neuk" and "Bonnie" meant in Scottish. Our family was English and Scottish. According to Wikipedia, Bonnie means "Good, pretty, or attractive" and Neuk means "corner or nook." She must have translated it to mean the "Good Corner." Fascinating. I will name my tea room Victoria Storm's Bonnie Neuk. Wait a minute. Am I going to open a tea room? Increasingly, it seems like a good business idea to pursue.

Returning to the library's front desk, I used their machine to copy the section of the book containing information about the tea room. I had copies of my dad's book, but they were packed away in my things somewhere. I knew he had written five books in all. I thanked Tammy for her help.

"Will we be seeing more of you in the future?" asked Tammy.

"Possibly. I might move back here. What do you think of a tea room in Metuchen?"

"Sounds wonderful! Any idea where you'd locate it? I love freshly brewed tea and maybe some homemade scones with Devonshire cream."

"I have no idea where I would open a tea room. I'm in the thinking stage."

"Mannon Realty is down the street on Middlesex Avenue. Check in with Richard. He's usually in the office and extremely helpful. Just stop in and ask."

"Mannon. That sounds like a familiar name from high school. I graduated in 1965."

"I think he graduated from MHS in either '63 or '64. I graduated in 1961 and never left town," stated Tammy. "I love this old town."

"I left many years ago but may decide to move back."

"Let me know more about the tea room as you work through things. Keep in touch, I'm interested."

"Did I hear something about a tea room?" asked Elizabeth Harp, the head librarian. "That would be a great idea. I'm sure the Borough Improvement League (BIL) and the Historical Society would love to hold events there. Keep me in the loop. By the way, I'm Liz," she said extending her hand in friendship.

Elizabeth (Liz) Harp appeared to be a matter-of-fact, no nonsense person. If she couldn't see it or touch it, it wasn't real. As I eventually learned, she had lived for more than forty years with this philosophy and it never failed her.

"I heard you mention a tea room. Are you going to open one near here?" inquired a lady checking out a few books. "Sounds like a good idea. We have a café here and several restaurants, but nothing resembling a tea room. That would be different and popular with the locals. I, for one, would love to come in."

I was encouraged by the positive feedback. "I'm thinking about it."

Fishing in her handbag, the lady gave me her card: Stacy Simms, Zumba instructor, YMCA. "Let me know as you work it through. I'd be happy to give advice if you decide to locate here. You might even like to join the YMCA and take a Zumba class. Or just get in touch with your inner self with yoga."

'Thanks, I appreciate that. I do Zumba now. I'd have to move here from Pennsylvania. Not all bad, mind you." I chatted a few more minutes about Zumba and other things happening in the town, then headed to my car. Maybe I would drive around and look for a store or a house for sale in town. I could find the phone number of Mannon Realty and begin a search for the right property.

I unlocked my car, checked my cell phone—two missed calls. I sat lost in thought for a moment. My phone startled me. *"The book helped, didn't it? The Bonnie Neuk; you hit the nail on the head! "* As before, the phone went dead. What was going on?

CHAPTER 3

"Drinking a daily cup of tea will surely starve the apothecary."
Chinese Proverb

It was still early in the afternoon. If I stopped at the Realtor, I could ask a few questions and then get a bite to eat. I drove to the office, parked, and entered a pleasant, airy room.

The receptionist asked my name and my concerns. I explained my requirements—a commercial property or home that I could convert into a tea room in the Main Street area, which was a mile long with several intersecting side streets. Many people have never experienced life in a small town.

"I can connect you with a Realtor shortly. Did you have an appointment?" I shook my head. "Richard Mannon should be off the phone in a moment; I'll put a note on his desk and let him know you're here."

After a few minutes I asked the receptionist if Richard had graduated from MHS. "Yes, he did, but I don't know what year."

Why was I sitting in a real estate office thinking about opening a tea room? What did I know about tea and it's discovery? Well, I had done some research. According to legend, the first cup of tea was discovered by the Chinese Emperor Shen Nung in 2737 BC. It is said that the emperor liked his drinking water boiled before he drank it, so it would be clean. One day, on a trip to a distant region, he and his army stopped to rest. A servant began boiling water when a dead leaf from the wild tea bush fell into the pot, turning the water a brownish color. But it went unnoticed and was presented to the emperor. The emperor drank it, found the liquid refreshing, and the cup of tea became part of Chinese cuisine. From China, the idea of "tea" spread throughout the world. It was introduced into the United States in 1650 by Peter Stuyvesant, who brought it to the colonists inhabiting New Amsterdam (now New York).

Iced tea was invented in 1904 at the St. Louis World's Fair, the same year teabags made their first commercial appearance. Today, iced tea is approximately 80 percent of the 140 million cups of tea ingested every day by Americans. Tea can also be used to stain fabric, make cold compresses for swollen eyes or extracted teeth, and soothe sunburns. As one of the four common sources of caffeine for Americans, 1.42 million pounds of tea are consumed daily in the U.S. I would have never guessed it is the most popular and cheapest beverage, next to water, in the world. An average of three billion cups of tea is consumed each day worldwide. There are four basic types—Black Tea, Green Tea, Oolong Tea, and Darjeeling tea, plus several types of tea-like drinks. There is Rooibos, a red tea grown only in South Africa, and herbal teas, which are infused with herbs, spices, and flowers. The tea leaf is from the <u>Camellia sinensis</u> plant. And there is pu erh tea, pronounced Poo-air and found in Yunnan, China. It is the most ancient of all teas, famous for its great taste and health benefits. It may help lower cholesterol levels, boost the flow of blood to increase circulation, and aid in proper digestion. Amazing! All that in one tea leaf.

My mental ramblings were interrupted by a masculine voice. "Hello, Victoria. I'm Richard Mannon. How can I help you?"

Richard was a handsome man who looked to be in his late forties. He definitely took care of himself. Maybe worked out at the gym. He presented an air of determination, combined with a bit of conceit. He stood tall and shook my hand with positive energy, appearing somewhat familiar to me. Did I remember him from high school?

"Sorry I didn't call for an appointment. I was in town and decided to make inquiries about properties in Metuchen. I'm considering moving back. It was home until I graduated from MHS in 1965 and then spent several years at Union Junior College. Were you the class of 1964 or 1963? You look like someone I knew in high school."

"Class of 1964," Richard said. "What was your maiden name?"

"Thorn. Seems a lifetime ago."

"Weren't you in the photography club and a member of the yearbook staff? I was in both and seem to remember you."

"Yes, I was in both clubs and still love to take photos. In fact, I minored in photography in college." I remembered him now. He went out with half his class and mine—a real lady's man. The conversation came to an abrupt halt. I needed to formulate what I was thinking and why I was here.

"I'm considering opening a tea room. During the 1930s

my grandmother had a tea room on Middlesex Avenue out by Bridge and Prospect. I would prefer a house or store for conversion to the tea room with an apartment on the top. I hope to buy rather than rent something either on Main Street or off one of the side streets. I need a central location with adequate parking."

"Let's see what the computer shows in terms of stores on Main Street; we'll look at the surrounding areas for houses that can be converted. Give me five minutes to search."

I walked back to the other room and sat down. The receptionist smiled and said, "I overheard you mention something about a tea room. We have a café here in town, but it serves mainly coffees and soda. And we have a Starbucks in Menlo Park, and there is a Teavana Store in Menlo Park Mall, too. They have this really neat wall of tins filled with teas. Over the last few years, people have been trying more tea and realizing how good it is for you. So many health benefits. Me, I've always loved tea."

"That's positive feedback. I hope to do special parties and caterings, as well as luncheons and tea parties. What's your name?"

"Betty Lou James. I've lived here all my twenty-six years. Can't wait until you open! I really do love tea," she repeated with enthusiasm.

Richard emerged from his office with a stack of papers, red hot from the Internet real estate site and multi-listings. "I haven't had lunch yet? Why don't we get a bite to eat? During lunch, I'll call the realtors and see if I can obtain keys or combinations to the lockboxes. We can talk about each place and narrow them down. There are nine possibilities—two stores and seven houses."

We walked around the corner and headed for the Duchess diner. I was suddenly flooded with old memories. The Duchess used to be the teenage hangout for Metuchen High students, who frequented the diner after dances.

"I'll have a BLT," said Richard. "What would you like?"

"A chicken Caesar." I turned to Richard to discuss the possibilities. "Some of these are too far outside of town." We narrowed it down to seven—two stores and five houses.

I looked at the pictures of the stores and neither seemed right. "If we could see them today, I could either rule them out or keep them under consideration." Several of the houses were in a good location, but only two appealed to me. Richard called the agents; we could see the stores this afternoon. The houses would have to wait for another day.

We spent the next hour looking at stat sheets, eating lunch and talking.

"Richard, both stores on Main Street are excellent locations, but too small. The tea room I envisioned would need a place for tables and chairs, a gift area, and a good-sized kitchen." One store didn't have an apartment. Richard made appointments for the houses. One was already under contract, but four were available. That fit my schedule. I had an appointment the next afternoon with Marie Pole. I could return to Metuchen the following day to check out the other properties.

"I'll set up appointments and afterwards we can have dinner at the Metuchen Inn." Richard suggested.

"That will work out perfectly. I can't remember my last visit to the Inn. Is it as quaint and charming as it used to be?"

"There was a fire at the Inn and it's undergone major renovations, but it has rustic ceiling beams and dark wood. There's a cozy bar and small areas upstairs for a banquet room."

"I'll meet you at your office around 1:30 on Thursday." I promised enthusiastically. I had a date! Wow, after twenty-five years I had a date. I had mixed emotions. Although disturbing, I promised myself to just enjoy his company with no thought of future entanglements. Life was to be explored and treasured. I had no desire to begin another relationship. Too soon, too sore, too new for me.

CHAPTER 4

*"I wish we could sit down together, and
have a cup of tea,
But since we can't,
When you have this one,
I hope you'll think of me."*
Author Unknown

Entering Maria's office was always a treat. Sage or basil or other spices permeated the air of her sitting room, enveloping clients with pleasant aromas and unusual fragrances. I sat on the sofa and closed my eyes. So relaxing. Having known Maria for forty years, we greeted each other warmly.

"There have been many changes in my life since the last time I saw you, which is why I am here. I've been lost since my divorce and searching, but still don't seem to have a direction,"

"Let's see what is happening and why. Let me have a piece of your jewelry." Maria requested.

"Maria, you have always asked for a piece of jewelry. Why do you do that? What do you call the type of psychic reading you do with my jewelry?" I asked.

"It is called Psychometry. I'll explain more in depth. Have you ever touched someone or something and received a message? Perhaps a picture or a word or two may have come to mind? Have you ever been shopping in an antique store and picked up an item at random—a tea cup or plate—and immediately formed an impression or image in your mind? If that is the case, you have experienced Psychometry. It is the art of interpreting the psychic vibrations contained in an object. It is sometimes referred to as 'psychic touch'—the ability to read an object's history."

"I know I have picked up a tea cup and immediately had a feeling of calm, sometimes even a feeling of confusion and sadness. Is that the psychic vibrations you're describing?"

"Exactly. It generally reflects the past, but it might call to mind a present or current situation," Maria said. "I have used it while working with the police to find a missing person. I can touch an object a person has worn or handled to experience an intuitive impression of his or her whereabouts. These items can reveal information things about the wearer, such as thoughts, emotional states, and significant events affecting their lives. In order to receive precise information about a situation, the object must belong to the person involved."

"That's interesting."

"It works most of the time. However, sometimes they are not found alive, which makes it hard to do this type of work."

She took my hand and we moved to her desk. I removed my ring and placed it in her palm.

"I am asking God to guide me for the truth and the light for Victoria Storm," asked Maria. Without hesitation she said, "I am predicting you will soon come into a considerable amount of money if you haven't already. I picture you undertaking a new endeavor. You will learn different things and make wonderful friends, but you will be living in a different area."

By way of explanation, she said, "Messages are subtle and gentle once contacts are made. If you properly tune in, spirit communication works. Become keenly observant. Avoid incorrect turns, wrong directions, and closed doors."

"How will I know?"

"If you encounter numerous roadblocks, your spirit guides are trying to warn you. Listen to their subtle clues. If you take the time to observe them, you will understand that someone is trying to tell you something! Perhaps you were not always listening. From my point of view, everything happens serendipitously. I don't believe in coincidence or fate. Our spirit guides draw us to what we need to learn. Many people ask me if our guides are with us all the time, or whether we have to reach out to them. We are never alone. Our guides are with us always. Their spiritual task is to watch over and assist us. But we never need to call them because they anticipate our needs. Do you understand?"

I took a deep breath. "I think...I do. So far, everything I have considered regarding the concept of this tea room has gone smoothly. There have been no roadblocks. Maybe it's supposed to happen."

"Listen to your guides, Victoria. Call me whenever you have questions," Maria said. "Sounds like you are moving to a new place; maybe it will be Metuchen."

I realized that this soul-destroying bitterness couldn't continue. As the saying goes, the best revenge was living well—pursuing a successful, independent life. So I would put my energy into a new venture—the tea room. And that is how it all started to fall into place and become a reality —The Bonnie Neuk Tea Room, of Metuchen, New Jersey. Lots to do, learn, and experience.

CHAPTER 5

"Love and scandal are the best sweeteners of tea."
Henry Fielding

On Thursday afternoon, I returned for my appointment with Richard Mannon to check out the last of the houses. We met at his office.

"There were two on Main Street. One house is past the post office toward Route 1. We'll look at that first," stated Richard.

We checked it out, but it seemed too small and too dreary for my thoughts of a tea room. Scratch one. We drove to the other. It had a few possibilities. Put one on the "maybe" list.

"There's another on Main Street."

As we drove up, I said," It is definitely too far away from the main flow of people and traffic." That left the remaining one on Middlesex.

25

As we swung into the driveway, I felt an immediate connection. It was a pale yellow house with a spacious white porch wrapping around to the side. I could envision two or three white New England rockers. There was a double white front door and numerous windows, insuring the rooms inside would be light and airy.

Reading from the Realtor's Sheet, Richard said "The main house has a foyer, large living with fireplace and dining room, as well as a kitchen and mud room in the back. There's a separate three-car garage in the rear with a small apartment above. Condition is listed as fair. The second floor has six bedrooms and three baths. There's a large room with kitchenette and bath on the third floor that was used as a small efficiency apartment."

We parked the car in the rear of the house. The back porch and patio were roomy, a perfect spot for a fountain and future garden. There was a porch area to set up tables outside when the weather was warmer. I could increase it so it could hold more tables. The plantings were old and sparse, but there was potential.

"Richard, the driveway is long with ample parking on the one side." Mentally, my wheels were already turning.

We walked to the front porch and unlocked the door. There on the jam was a penny—heads up. I felt as if the house was extending a warm greeting. Maria had said our spirit guides draw us to what we need. Definitely friendly vibes.

I took out my camera and said to Richard, "I'm going to take some photos inside and outside—the garden what there is of it—and the porch. Lots of nooks and crannies."

We walked into a spacious foyer with two rooms on either side. There was a lovely stone fireplace in the living room; both it and a large dining room had hardwood floors. The kitchen was a good size with many windows and an ample pantry off to the side. A small mud room with bathroom led to the back porch. It could become a functional tea-room kitchen. The house could easily be converted into a lovely tea room—The Bonnie Neuk. We went upstairs to check out the bedrooms, then the third floor, and out to the garage apartment. I was snapping photos the entire time.

Thoughts and ideas were spinning in my head. "Give me a little time to absorb all of this and we'll chat more later, Richard. I'd like to wander around the house by myself and feel the ambiance of each space. Maybe you could just hang out for a little while."

I spent over an hour going from room to room, taking photos, and exploring various spaces. Honestly, I didn't want to leave, but my stomach was growling so loud, I'm sure it was noticeable. Richard suggested we head out to dinner where we could chat about what I had seen.

Returning to his car, Richard drove us to the Metuchen Inn for dinner. I had fallen in love with 457 Middlesex Avenue. It would be the best place to open the tea room, as it was close to town with ample parking. If I needed additional parking, maybe I could negotiate with the neighbors on the left to use a little of their space since it was a house doctor's office.

Unfortunately, the price of the house was more than I wanted to spend, considering the numerous renovations I would have to do, as well as the permits and zoning requirements. We discussed our plan.

"I feel you could offer less. It was an estate sale and had been on the market for over eight months," explained Richard. "Besides, there are rumors that a ghost haunts the place. But who believes that! All the owners have to do is negotiate a price higher than we offered. Let's try."

During dinner, Richard asked my impressions about the houses and my feelings in terms of moving back to Metuchen. I enjoyed a glass of white wine; he had gin on the rocks. Since I had a lengthy drive back to Pennsylvania, one was my limit. Richard was on his third. It

27

was early, around 7:00 pm, when we finished dinner and coffee.

As we drove back to his office, I said "Thanks for the meal and the talk about the plans for an offer and local contacts with a contractor and architect. I'd like to put the offer on hold until I meet with my children on Saturday to discuss my possible plans and do some serious thinking. We'll talk early next week."

As I exited his car and was heading toward mine, Richard moved toward me. Unexpectedly, he put the full force of his body against mine. I couldn't move. He kissed me with such force that it took my breath away—not in a good way. Had I said something to lead him on? Seconds later, he attempted to unbutton my blouse. It took me a moment to react. I've never been a prude, but this was far too early and completely out of line.

Pulling his hand away, I responded angrily, "A kiss, to say nothing of a frontal attack, is not part of this deal. You haven't changed since high school, have you! You were a sex starved creep back then. If you do not stop, I will knee you, do you understand me?"

He hung his head and moved back. "I'm sorry. I thought you would enjoy a little kiss and some fun."

"A kiss might have been acceptable, but the groping was totally inappropriate. I am not in the market for either a fling or a physical relationship. I would enjoy going out for a movie or dinner, but that's all. Do you understand?" I questioned firmly. My insides were turning into an angry knot.

"You've made yourself quite clear. No hard feelings, I hope," Richard responded with a weak smile.

"We need to keep this on a business basis. I hope to purchase the house through your agency and hope that I can count on your support with negotiation. Let's remain friends." I turned around, got into my car, and sped away. Just what I needed—an unexpected physical attack by my realtor. I drove home in an irritated mood. Was I ready for this kind of social scene? No way. No how, not now.

CHAPTER 6

"The shortest distance between two strangers is a full teapot and two cups."
Author unknown

I had a direction for my future and was ready to spring into action. I did a computer search for the Building Department in Metuchen, compiled a list of all officials and their phone numbers, and immediately called the construction officer, Brad Randal, to determine procedures regarding renovations. We made an appointment for the following Monday at 11:00 to discuss my building requirements. Brad recommended a Perry Jones for my architect and gave me his number. He explained that Perry had a great eye for taking what was originally built and creating something better. I called and made an appointment for the same Monday afternoon at 2:00.

"I can also recommend a landscape architect. His name

is Hilliard McDonald, and his number is 555-1212," said Brad, "Use my phone."

My call was to make an appointment for him to drive by the house, check out the backyard, and discuss ideas. He said he would meet me on Monday. I explained to him about the garden and fountain plans. He rejected the English garden idea. His remark was that it was too busy for the small space. A bit pompous, but what do I know? He agreed to take measurements and rough out the area on paper. Things were moving forward.

"Hello, may I speak to Chris Checks, the president of the zoning board, please. This is Victoria Storm." The receptionist put me on hold.

"Hello, Ms. Storm. Chris Checks here. How may I help you?

"I am purchasing a house on Middlesex Avenue to convert into a tea room. I wanted to discuss the zoning requirements and what paperwork is needed. Would you have a few minutes on Monday around noon? I have an appointment with Brad Randal at 11:00."

"Why don't I come by Brad's office at the end of your meeting and we'll discuss this together. My office is next to his,"

"That will work well. See you on Monday."

It would be a busy Monday, but busy is good.

Richard had given me the names of two contractors, Tom Crown and Ron Metter, as well as a landscape architect, Hilliard McDonald, to design the water garden. That made two recommendations for McDonald.

I wanted this all in place when my offer was accepted and before settlement, which is usually in six weeks. The work could be started right away, figuring it would take ten to twelve weeks to finish the renovations and all the changes on the house, then begin improvements on the garage apartment. My plan was to complete the bedrooms first, move into the third floor and oversee the work in the kitchen and tea room area and finally the garage. I could then begin selecting items for decorating the tea room. Can't believe I'm doing this.

My phone rang, *"Don't forget to find a place in the tea room for Mr. Ted Bear, like your Grandma."* As usual, the phone went dead. Who keeps calling me and hanging up? And how do they know something about my bear? I didn't even know that Mr. Ted Bear was in my grandmother's tea room. I need to call several of my parents' friends to see if they remembered anything about the bear. They are old, so I hope they remember something. But first on my list is to find out who keeps calling me. I don't understand how they know these little bits of information about me or my grandmother. Time to check with Verizon and learn how to trace a call. I dialed 611 on my cell and asked the operator "Does the number and/or name of the caller show up on the phone?"

She replied, "Only names in your phone contacts list will appear on your screen. People can restrict their numbers." That didn't provide much help.

In the interim, I wanted to sit with my children and explain what their mother was doing and the dream she was following. They would support me in any venture, but I've always valued their opinions and recommendations. That's what families do. I scheduled dinner at Lai Lai, a Japanese restaurant, for Saturday night. After our talk, I'd call Richard to discuss the offer.

CHAPTER 7

"Just Tea for Two and Two for Tea.
Just Me for You and You for Me."
Irving Caesar, *"Tea for Two"*

Spending time with my children is always a good experience. And dinner when mother is paying is even better from their point of view. My kids knew I had left their father and was renting an apartment in Willow Grove, Pennsylvania. More significantly, they understood I was working my way through new life changes.

I had chosen a quiet sushi restaurant. My daughter, Ann and her husband, Frank, were the first to arrive. We ordered a bottle of wine and did some catching up. Adam came next, with Anthony and Lauri right behind him. It was a treat to be together again. The first bottle of wine didn't go far, so we ordered a second and a third.

I suggested, "Let's try Japanese green seaweed salads,

miso soup, and an assortment of tuna, eel, yellow tail and California rolls with plenty of sliced pickled ginger."

"Sounds great!" Ann answered. The sushi would take some time to prepare as items are made fresh. We chatted over some Japanese chips and sweet and sour sauce.

"There is some news I need to discuss with all of you," I began, taking a deep breath. "I have been searching for a new career. What do you think about me moving back to Metuchen and opening a tea room? In 1932 my grandmother had a tea room in town called The Bonnie Neuk. Since I need a new direction for my life, something about her idea appeals to me. Opening a tea room is a consideration."

Simultaneously, they all picked up their wine glasses and toasted me.

"Mom, it sounds like a great idea. Too bad your grandmother isn't here to give you some advice," Ann pointed out.

Adam said, "Sounds like an interesting venture, one that could become a success."

"Knowing you, I'm sure you've done your homework and have learned all about teas and their preparation. I, myself, love tea and can't wait to try some of your interesting blends. My concern is that this is a big and expensive venture. Are you sure it will be successful?" Anthony asked.

"Y-e-s, I've been doing a bit of research online. I've found two great tea distributors—Rishi Tea and Tea Fonte, both offering a wide variety of unique teas shipped days after the harvest. I've spent a few days in Metuchen checking out locations. I talked with many people, businesses, community organizations, and clubs to have feedback. Nothing in life is foolproof. I'll move forward with positive energy." I passed around a packet of photos I had taken of the house. They all agreed it looked like a perfect place with future possibilities of a bed and breakfast.

"Okay, Mom, it sounds like you're on top of things. My one concern is how you'll find dependable staff," commented Ann. "I'd love to help out for awhile. Maybe I can take a week's vacation when the time comes."

"That would be great. I plan to advertise a few weeks before opening to interview for waitresses, pastry chefs, and other staff. But I hear what you're saying about finding someone reliable. It's not easy. I'd love to have your help."

"Maybe I could take a week off at a different time and help out," said Adam. "That way you would have two weeks covered. Anthony, could you spare a week?"

"Maybe I could do a few weekends. I started this new job, but I don't think they'd mind if I left a little early on Fridays. We'll work this out, Mom. We have you covered for the week before and after opening."

"Opening date is up in the air, but I should have a rough idea shortly. The renovation should take three months and the garage apartment a month more. Living in the house for a short time will allow me to oversee the work. When the garage apartment has been completed, I'll move in."

"We'll drive over to see the house in the next few weeks," said Adam.

"That would be super. I'll get new perspective and ideas. Let me know when you can spare a few hours and I'll make arrangements." Later, getting into my car, I saw something on the ground reflecting the light. I stooped down and picked up a shiny penny—heads up.

CHAPTER 8

"All true tea lovers not only like their tea strong, but like it a little stronger with each year that passes."
George Orwell. *"A Nice Cup of Tea"*

As I drove to Metuchen on Monday, I called Richard on my Bluetooth to schedule a time to pick up the keys. "Richard, what do you feel we should offer for the house?"

"I feel $440,000 would be a starting offer. I'll make the offer on Tuesday and wait to hear from the sellers. That's the hard part."

"While waiting for their reply, can you help me apply for a small mortgage with the local bank? Maybe Wells Fargo. My estimate for the renovations ranges between $250,000 to $350,000, which would leave me with a good chunk of change left over. I have several appointments today: the construction officer and building inspector, Mr. Randell, at 11:00; the zoning officer, Mr. Checks at 12:00; the architect Perry Jones at 2:00; and maybe Hil-

liard McDonald after that. Busy day!"

"Sounds like it. But I'm sure it will be productive."

"I've called Tom Crown, the contractor that you suggested, and left another message with his receptionist about a possible appointment today or Friday. She said she'd have him get back to me."

The Borough Hall had a long aisle with names on the office doors. I knocked on the one marked "Construction Officer," and heard a voice holler "come in".

"Hello, Mr. Randell, Victoria Storm. I'm planning to open a tea room on Middlesex Avenue and will be doing some renovations. I'll need some advice. I've come to pick your brain."

"Hello, Victoria. You'll need to discuss some deadlines and the inspection that will be needed to complete the reconstruction's pecking order. Who are you using as your contractor? He'll do the set up for the inspections."

"I'm trying to make an appointment with Tom Crown and a second recommendation with Ron Metter."

"Both are equally capable."

I called Crown again after my meeting with Mr. Randell. Maybe busy is good. Through his receptionist, arrangements were made to meet on Friday at the house.

My next appointment was with Chris Checks, the zoning officer. "Hello, Mr. Checks, I'm Victoria Storm. I'm purchasing the house and will be transforming it into a tea room."

"How do you do, Victoria. You're the tea room lady I've heard so much about. Congratulations. That sounds like a great addition to the Metuchen restaurant scene, something different. Here are some of the things you'll need." He handed me a few sheets of paper. "I'll be working with your contractor. Who have you chosen?"

"I have two in mind, and I have a meeting Friday with Tom Crown. I have a meeting today after our appointment with Perry Jones."

Before I could explain that he was going to be my architect, Mr. Checks enthusiastically said, "You'll love him. He can put your ideas down on paper with ease and style. I don't know much about Crown."

"I'm having Hilliard McDonald do some landscape work in the rear of the house, since I'm planning a small garden with a fountain."

"He's equally knowledgeable and easy to work with. He knows his stuff. Your tea room will be an eating and drinking establishment. You and your contractor will need to write up a proposal that should address such things as how many tables you plan to have and how many people you can accommodate, which will determine parking. You will need a building permit, but your contractor can see to that. Your architect will need to submit a design and plans. You will need the Health Department to make several inspections, including one after you've opened."

I talked to him about the possibility of getting permission from my neighbors to use some of their parking area. It seems I would need to send a proposal to the zoning board to obtain a variance. However, he didn't think that would be a big hurdle.

"You'll need to submit signage and color information. There are restrictions on color in the downtown area, as well as the size of the sign."

All in all, it was an informative meeting, well worth my time. It was nearly 1:30. I had a few minutes to run into the Duchess Diner, grab a quick salad, and call Liz before my meeting with Perry.

"Hi Liz, Victoria Storm. I was in a week ago looking

41

for my father's book in the basement."

"Yes, I remember. How's it going with the tea room?"

"It's coming along surprisingly well. I'm going to be in Metuchen all day meeting with the contractor for the house renovations and a contractor for the garden in the rear. I thought it would be fun to get together later for martinis, food, and conversation at the Metuchen Inn. Maybe Tammy can join us. I'd like to know both of you better."

"What a great idea," agreed Liz.

"You ask Tammy and I'll meet both of you at the Inn at 5:30. I'll try calling Stacy at the YMCA and see if she'd like to come."

I picked up the keys and arrived at the house before two, parked my car, and entered through the back door. I watched as Perry Jones pulled up. He was unusually tall and thin, with big delphinium blue eyes, long blond hair to below his ears, and was dressed casually in khakis and a golf shirt.

I met him at the back door. "Hello, Mr. Jones, I'm Victoria Storm. Nice to meet you." I extended my hand.

"Hello, Victoria. Call me Perry. Lovely house you have here." Getting right to the point he said, "What are your plans?"

"I'll be officially purchasing the house in several weeks. I plan to make the downstairs into a tea room." I handed him a list of my requirements and explained what I envisioned. "The gift shop will be located immediately inside the front door. I want a small wall to display hats and accessories. The two rooms, the actual living and dining room, will have seating for forty people with fifteen tables. The kitchen needs to be bright, with stainless steel sinks around the two walls, a double refrigerator and single freezer, two ovens, a large microwave on the third wall, and a long counter on the other. The pantry will require numerous shelves from floor to ceiling. The mud room should have a small bathroom and an area off to the side for employees. I envision the front porch continuing around to the back, which would allow customers to walk around to a lovely garden and porch area. The inside walls would feature white clapboard on the bottom, with a pale sage on the top. The downstairs baths can remain as it is, with a facelift."

He looked around, and nodded in agreement. We walked off measurements, talked about the ambiance and space of certain areas, discussed windows and walls. Upstairs, the existing windows will insure plenty of light. Proceeding to the third floor, I suggested an updated small kitchen and living area. The bedroom and bath were adequate, but they needed a little updating, fresh paint, and new flooring.

"This is the final list for everything?" he asked.

"No, there's a garage apartment in the back that I'd like to upgrade with several walls added." We headed outside toward the garage apartment. "This is going to be my new home. I figured this way it would be separate from the tea room and possibly the future B and B, yet close to everything. I grew up here and left when I was eighteen. My maiden name was Thorn."

We continued to discuss plans. "It sounds like a super idea, curling up on the sofa with a good book, fuzzy slippers, and a cup of Rooibos tea. My idea of heaven," said Perry.

"That's one of my favorite teas, too." I said with a broad smile.

"I can't wait until your tea room opens. I'll be the first customer. I l-o-v-e t-e-a.

When do you need the plans?"

"I'd like to start work on the house the day after settlement, which is six weeks away. Could I have something in the next week to review with the contractor?"

"Yes, I could have the preliminaries to you by next week. The formal ones needed for submission might take a little longer."

"That will work out fine. Thanks for your time, Perry. It was a pleasure to meet you." I turned to walk away.

"Silly question," said Perry. "Are you related to the old gentleman who had the farm on High Street? We always went there for sweet yellow corn. It was so-o good."

"Yes, that was my great uncle Les Thorn. It was quite a farm. I used to sit alongside him on the tractor, picking corn, sorting in bags of six, then leaving it on his front porch. It was based on the honor system. Not sure it would work today."

Perry and I chatted in regard to ideas for the house and things we remembered about the town. He understood décor and living style and had an eye for using what was already there and improving on it. Already, he felt like an old friend. I went to the kitchen to pick up my purse and notebook. It wasn't there. I'm getting forgetful in my old age. I searched the main floor, then found it in the upstairs bathroom on the toilet tank. Why would I have put it there?

We left around 4:30, which meant I would have a little time to cruise around town to check things out before drinks and appetizers at the Inn. This was going to be my hometown again. It brought a smile to my face and a lightness in my heart.

Looking back at what was to become my home, I felt such a sense of pride. I was beginning a wonderful endeavor—one that I knew would eventually be a success. I got in my car and checked my messages. Tom Crown's receptionist confirmed he could meet me on Friday at the house at 9:30. It was time to drive to the Inn for drinks and appetizers with the "ladies." What fun!

CHAPTER 9

*"Let us gather for a greeting
With our teacups filled with tea
And I'll tell you how important
Your friendship is to me."*
Alda Ellis, *"Hats off to Tea"*

I sat in the car thinking about my new-found friends. They were all different, but each one wanted to support the other in their own endeavors. Tammy was upbeat, energetic, and always ready to try something new and exciting to add to her life—not a wallflower in the least. She was about five-foot-eight with long brown hair that she usually pulled back with a scrunchie. She was spiritual and always looking for answers from the universe. Liz was the opposite. She was set in her ways and needed concrete proof of things. She wasn't open to new things and resisted trying them. Stacy was the athletic one with her Zumba and YMCA training. She loved to push herself in work and in life. She was open to new things and new experiences. We made an interesting conglomeration of

45

women, but all with the idea of friendship and supporting one another in things that we each found important. I was enjoying them as friends, respecting each one with her own philosophy.

I walked into the Inn around 5:15 and sat at the bar. Under the bar stool, I spied a shiny penny—heads up. *Hi, Mom, love you too.* The three ladies hadn't arrived, but it was relaxing to sit for a few moments after a busy day. My mind wandered back to the last encounter I had at the Metuchen Inn, but I quickly decided not to go there. What was over was over.

As I looked around, I noticed the bar was crowded with gentlemen in suits and ties. I've always thought a man looked great with a bright colored shirt and colorful tie. These men were no exceptions. There must have been fifteen all in one area at the end of the bar. I thought there is definitely a group of good looking gentlemen in Metuchen these days. As I glanced toward them, I thought I recognized Perry Jones, but I wasn't sure. I'd left him over an hour ago and this was only a quick glance. Suddenly, they all stood up and went into a room in the back of the restaurant. Was it me? Did I have bad breath?

I asked the bartender what was going on. He told me it was a joining-commitment ceremony for two men and all their friends who were participating in the ceremony.

I had little time to react, as I spotted Tammy and Liz walking in. I waved to them from the bar.

"How's the progress on the tea room?" asked Liz with excitement in her voice.

"It was a busy day. I met with Richard to set up settlement; we offered $440,000. I guess I won't hear until Monday or Tuesday. All other meetings went well. I want everything to be in place before settlement. Then we'll begin work, tackling the tea room and main house first, leaving the garage apartment for last. I'll move into the third floor in the house for a few months until the garage is completed. Liz, could you do me a favor and do a brief research project on the owners and history of the house? I'd like to know who owned it and lived there and anything else you can find."

"Sure thing. It shouldn't take me long. The historical society had written a book and taught a course on 'researching your house' several years ago. I took it for fun. I should be able to find something. I'll check their newsletter, *Nannygoats*, for other information."

"Maybe the house is haunted and you'll find out," suggested Tammy with a giggle and a wicked smile. "You never know about those things!"

"There are no such things as ghosts," Liz said emphatically.

"I wouldn't be so sure of that, my dear," retorted Tammy. "The Ayer-Allen house is said to be haunted and has several ghosts residing there on a permanent basis. If I'm not mistaken, one is a soldier and one an American Indian. I know more than you do. Ghosts want to communicate with the living, but they want to help us, not scare us. Since they have not yet entered into the light, they are caught between the death's dimension and the spiritual realm. A ghost is an energy field that makes its presence known periodically in the same area, giving the awareness of a living person. A ghost brings a drop in temperature with its presence, perceived clairvoyantly as a fluffy, transparent human-like mass, moving slowly."

"You seem to know quite a bit about ghosts, Tammy," I replied. "I should do a little research myself on the subject. You said the Ayer-Allen house has several ghosts?'

"I've been looking into their existence for some time," explained Tammy.

"Hogwash, there are no such things as ghosts, ever," reaffirmed Liz.

At that moment, Stacy walked in and greeted everyone with a hug, ending our conversation on ghosts—at least for the time being. We moved to a table where we could chat—a regular ladies night out with laughter and fun. I hope we weren't disturbing their wedding. Inevitably, I mentioned the episode with Richard. They weren't shocked. Apparently, after a few drinks he becomes an overbearing ladies' man—a real womanizer.

"You guys could have warned me," I responded in an angry, teasing voice.

"He's harmless and just needs to be put in his place. And you sure did a good job of that," said Liz with a chuckle and a smile.

Tammy took me aside and whispered, "Did you know there are several applications you can put on a smart phone to find ghosts—Ghost Speaker, Ghost Detector, and Ghost Radar Classis, which I have on mine. You can try it with me anytime." I looked at her with surprise. Wow, you can hunt ghosts on your smart phone. Remembering I had a dumb phone, I smiled and nodded. Maybe I should upgrade my dumb phone for one of the new iPhones. Soon.

Stacy spoke up and suggested, "Why don't you stay at my place overnight and leave in the morning? That way you're not on the road late and you can enjoy another drink."

"You don't mind?" Finishing up the last morsels of vegetables and calamari, we ordered coffee, tea and dessert. "Thanks, I appreciate your offer. It's seems a longer drive each time I do it."

"Anytime you need a place to crash for the night, call me. I'm by myself and it's no trouble," Stacy said.

"I may take you up on that several times in the future."

Turning to my new friends, I told them about my project. "Ladies, I'll be taking a course and doing tasseography, which is reading tea leaves. There will be a Tarot card reader once a week or every other week. Don't laugh. I've completed a class in the basics of reading the leaves. I think my grandmother used to read them and I also think she read palms. At least that was what I'm led to believe. I bet she sometimes read them in her tea room. I figured I'd read the leaves periodically, perhaps hiring someone from town to read the cards, or maybe learn myself. Who knows? Maybe I'll even wear a sheer shirt and a hip scarf with coins that jangle. That should have me looking the part of a gypsy."

"Fascinating ideas," Liz said skeptically. "Of course it's just for entertainment and not for real."

"You need to have leaves in your cup in order to read them correctly? How does that work? I make tea with bags. " Tammy commented.

"Show us. Read my tea leaves. Please," asked Stacy.

"I'm not sure how good I am at it yet, but I can practice on the three of you. Let's see if the restaurant can fix us a teapot filled with hot water. I have some Earl Grey tea and my cheat sheet for the meaning of some of the symbols."

I ran to the car to retrieve my leaves and my tasseography notebook. Returning, I put three teaspoons plus one for the pot in the teapot. "I have to 'Make like a Tree,' which means figuratively to put your roots down deep in the earth for grounding." I took three deep cleansing breaths and cleared my body and mind from my toes to my head, allowing the white light to come in. "Spirits need to be able to use me as a means of bringing the messages. You always need to protect yourself from evil spirits and wrap yourself in the white light."

"What do we do now?" Stacy asked.

"We need to drink the tea, being careful not to swallow many loose leaves. Put your teeth together and use them as a block. That's the tricky part— the challenge of drinking the tea and not the leaves. Allow a small amount of liquid, a drop or two, to remain in the bottom of the cup. Turn the cup over onto the saucer, revolve it three times

clockwise, and turn it back upright. Then we'll examine the tea leaves. It's somewhat similar to looking at the sky and imagining figures and signs in the clouds. There are three time periods the leaves will reveal. From the rim of the cup to the top of the handle are things in the immediate present and near future. The area from the top of the handle to the bottom of the handle (or the middle area) is for periods of approximately three months. The area from the bottom of the handle to the bottom of the cup represents a time frame of up to a year."

"Can you tell me about the past?" Tammy asked.

"No, the leaves only predict your future."

"Do me first," Stacy requested. "I'll count the turns of the cup; one, two, and three." She turned the cup upright and I looked into it to see what was forming.

"On the side of the cup near the middle, I could see a bird, which indicates good news in the next few weeks to several months. On the bottom of the cup, I detect a heart and next to it, a tree." As I looked that up in my notebook, I said, "The heart symbolizes finding love or meeting someone you can trust. The tree means improvements either to oneself or to your surroundings. Some of the other leaves don't seem to represent anything to my eyes. Remember, I'm green at this. I just took the class."

"That seems accurate. I have decided to take some night classes at Middlesex College in the fall. And I think I've found someone I can trust—you," said Stacy.

"Do mine next." interjected Tammy. "One, two, three," and she turned the cup over in the saucer.

"There is a snake in the far corner of the cup. Snakes can be an enemy, but they can also indicate wisdom or the possibility of learning something new. My feelings direct me that something new would be significant. On the upper part of the cup is a chair or seat, meaning you will have a guest or someone visiting. And in the rim area, which indicates the near future, I see an anchor representing constancy or stability."

"I may be expecting my mother for a visit in the next few weeks. She lives in Ohio," Tammy responded.

"Okay, Liz, do you want yours read?' I asked.

"I'll wait on that. I'm not a believer in things like this." Liz turned her nose up in the air in disapproval.

"That was great fun," said Stacy. "I think it will become popular at the Bonnie Neuk. People always enjoy learning about their future."

"Don't know about all of you, but I'm tired." I said yawning. "Let's pay the bill and get some sleep."

It had been an enjoyable evening. I learned more about my new friends as they did about me, a foundation on which to build strong friendships. I'd spend the night in Metuchen, certainly better than driving back to Pennsylvania.

CHAPTER 10

"If you are cold, tea will warm you;
If you are too hot, it will cool you;
If you are depressed, it will cheer you;
If you are exhausted, it will calm you."
William Gladstone

After picking up the key at Richard's office on Friday, I waited at the house, considering various options while enjoying the panoramic view of the living and dining room areas. At 9:30 Tom still hadn't shown up, and at 9:45 he had yet to appear or call. I called his receptionist, who said his schedule indicated he'd be in Perth Amboy all day.

At this point I had had enough of Tom Crown. What had Maria Pole said? "Read the subtle clues your spirit guides are trying to warn you." I indicated no further interest to the receptionist. I dialed Ron Metter, expecting to leave a message. Ron answered on the third ring. "Home Renovation, Inc., may I help you?" Amazingly, he answers his own phone.

"Victoria Storm, Mr. Metter. I'm undertaking an extensive renovation of a house on Middlesex Avenue in Metuchen. Is there a time we could meet to discuss the plans? Maybe today? I know its short notice." I laughed to myself, instant meetings just don't happen.

"I'm on a job right now, getting my team started. Could I meet you around noon at the house. And call me Ron. What's the address?"

"457 Middlesex. I'll see you there." *What a difference! Maria, you are so right. The spirits are showing me.* With several hours to kill, I opted for thrift store shopping. I had many things to find, either used or abused. Suddenly my phone rang. Damn, Ron was canceling. *"The house would look lovely in a light sage for the walls and white on the trim and railings."* As usual, the phone went dead. This time I shouted into the receiver. "I was already planning to use light sage with white. Who are you?" Of course, no one answered me. I felt like a fool yelling into the phone. Who was making these calls? Someone was having fun and playing a joke. It was starting to freak me out.

I pulled into the parking lot and entered the thrift store. The lady at the counter spoke to me. "Hello, I'm Nellie. May I help you in any way?"

"Hi, Victoria Storm. I'm looking for tea cups, plates, and silverware."

"Are you the lady who is opening the tea room on Middlesex Avenue?" Nellie inquired with a big smile.

"Unbelievable how fast news travels in a small town. Yes, I am."

"What an interesting idea. I'm sure many of the clubs and organizations will plan some of their events at your place. You'll need to get the word out."

"I hope to open toward the middle or end of August. I'll start slow, and then increase the time and events as the tea room becomes known. At present, I'm in the planning stages."

"We have some odd cups and saucers in the back room and a few linen tablecloths. I have a box of stuff in the garage. If you wait a few minutes, I'll bring them in."

I walked up and down the aisles examining several pitchers, various pieces of silverware, a pile of linens with hand embroidering on the edges. I knew tea could be used to give the linens an antique look. Nellie returned minutes later with a large box. She motioned for me to look inside. The contents included twenty or twenty-five tea cups and saucers. Although all were mismatched, they were definitely colorful and dainty.

"Nellie, this is great! I'll take them all, as well as these." I handed her a pile of things I'd chosen. "How much do you want for everything?"

"Give me thirty-five dollars and we'll call it a day, but you have to invite me to come to the tea room as soon as you're open for business."

"The local paper will announce my opening. Please come." I handed her the cash, put the items in the car, and drove back to the house. What a good day! Only one small hiccup with Tom Crown, but that was for the best. Someone that undependable wouldn't finish the house in a timely manner. I was listening to my spirits, as Marie had suggested. Would Ron meet my expectations? He will, I know.

I had almost an hour before our meeting. I wanted to stop at the Borough Hall and speak to the police chief. I'd met him at one of my many meetings to discuss zoning, signage, and plan presentation.

"Hello Officer Stone, I'm Victoria Storm and I'm opening the new tea room. We met a week ago. I need to pick your brain regarding some cell phone calls I've been receiving. Do you have a minute?"

"I know cell phone marketing can be annoying, but there's not much you can do about it. You can put your number on the Do Not Call List."

"These are more than just marketing prank calls."

"Are they soliciting or threatening?"

"They're none of those. I'm not sure how I'd classify them besides mysterious. Someone calls and gives me little tidbits of knowledge for my tea room, then hangs up."

"My first suggestion would be to call your carrier and ask them to block the phone number.

Unless of course, it's someone that knows you and will try another line."

"The problem is there's no number or data displayed. I can't trace the call or block it because I don't have a phone number."

"That's odd. You're right, Verizon can't block it without a number. Not sure how they're doing that. My other suggestion would be to change your number. In that way, they would not find your new number."

"I never thought of that, but I've had the number for a long time and don't want to change it. I appreciate your help. Thanks." He sounded as perplexed as I, but I think a new smart phone is in order.

I arrived at the house a little before noon. Ron Metter from Home Renovation, Inc. was sitting on the back stoop with his notebook in one hand and a sandwich in the other. I extended my hand and said "Hello, I'm Victoria. You must be Ron Metter. I hope I didn't keep you waiting long."

"I'm sorry, I was sitting here eating my lunch and looking around the site, but sometimes there just isn't enough time to eat.

"Ron, please, continue eating."

"I figured it will take us an hour and I have to be at another job after that." Apologizing, he changed gears in a flash and started questioning me about the house.

"Who's the architect?"

"I'm using Perry Jones."

"He's great. When can I have the plans?"

"He promised to have the preliminaries by the middle of the week and the final ones to present to the board by the following week."

"Perfect timing. Let's walk through the house. You tell me what you and Perry talked about. What I'd like to do is understand your general ideas and visions as we go into each room. Once I see the plans, I'll be able to create a list of supplies. What kind of time frame are you looking at?" he asked.

"Settlement is mid April. I've made an offer and should have an answer by Monday. As soon as I've a closing date, I'll let you know. Hopefully, you could start the next day. I'd like to open mid August. Does that all sound feasible?"

"Let's see what has to be done. I have several teams I can put on the job. I'm sure we can work around that time frame." As we walked through each room, I explained about the friendly atmosphere I wanted to prevail throughout the Bonnie Neuk. We talked colors and wall textures, flooring, and windows. He felt the hardwood floors would all come up nicely with a light sanding. There was a small area in the dining room that had a little rot and needed to be replaced. We discussed my ideas for the gift shop and the entrance to the tea room. Unquestionably, I needed some professional advice regarding the kitchen. Most of it had to be gutted, replaced by new counters, appliances, stainless steel shelves, and tile flooring. Ron gave me some suggestions as we discussed the light I wanted and the restoration of the existing windows. Did I want all new tile and fixtures in the bathroom? Yes, updated and modern looking. The powder room in the hall would be the main bathroom for the tea room. It, too, needed to be gutted and the fixtures replaced, but it had ample room for a large sink area and toilet. I was having one rest room given the number of seats in the tea room.

The back bathroom was smaller and needed updating, but suitable for employees to use.

"I have an old stained glass window. We could install it in the back and make it look rather quaint," suggested Ron with a smile.

"That sounds interesting. Could I check it out first?" I asked.

Moving upstairs, we discussed the conversion of one of the bedrooms into two bathrooms. All the rooms had to have wallpaper removed and I wanted them to be painted. The third floor also needed to be updated with fresh paint. I'd live there while renovations were being completed in the rest of the house. Then there would be the garden area concept I had envisioned with a pond and garden. Hopefully Mr. McDonald would suggest some excellent ideas.

"Is that the extent of all we need to renovate?" asked Ron.

"No, there is an apartment over the garage that needs some help. Let's walk over and take a look." It started to mist a little, so walking to the garage ended in a mad dash.

"Green appliances, I thought they went out twenty years ago. Ugh!" commented Ron. He quickly glanced at me in case he had said something wrong and I wanted to keep the green ugly things.

"I couldn't agree with you more." We discussed the addition of walls, renovating the kitchen and cabinet area, removal of the wall paper and applying fresh paint. He gave me several cards to check out vendors for the kitchen cabinets and bathroom appliances along with a card for stainless steel counter tops.

"This is going to be a big job. Probably will take two months to three months to complete," Ron said.

"I would like you to work on the second and third floor first. I can live in the third floor as you are working on the rest of the house. When the house is completed, you'll work on the garage apartment –my eventual home."

"I'll start with one team on the house, since you indicated settlement was mid April. When most things are completed in the house, I'll move them over to the garage. I could have a second team, who are at a job currently, start work the beginning of May."

"As soon as Mr. Jones delivers the preliminary plans, let me have a set and we can once again go over the items. I'll need 20 percent down, let say $40,000, to purchase materials to start."

"I figured next week I'd bring a check to my contractors. I've discussed my plans with the township. They recommended you highly."

"I'll need the plans to submit and apply for permits from the township," stated Ron. We agreed to stay in touch. It was a productive meeting. I was more than satisfied with my new choice of contractors. Thanks, Marie. You were correct on things going smoothly.

CHAPTER 11

*"Peter was not very well during the evening.
His mother put him to bed and made some
chamomile tea. One tablespoon to be taken at
bed time."*
Beatrice Potter, *The Tale of Peter Rabbit.*

We didn't hear back from the sellers until late that Friday. Richard called with their counter offer of $450,000. We discussed what the best tactic would be. We decided on $447,000, but the offer couldn't be made until Monday morning. A weekend in limbo.

On Monday afternoon, my heart skipped a beat when I heard Richard's voice. "You got the house for $447,000. It's all yours."

My heart was pounding. "When is the closing scheduled?"

"We set it for six weeks, April 15. I've heard from Wells Fargo. You've been approved for $380,000, but there are a few other documents you'll need to supply."

"Thanks, Richard." Wells Fargo requested copies of my

driver's license and divorce decree. They would email me the good faith estimate and a few other mortgage documents and confirm the settlement date of April 15.

I called Ron to give him the closing date on the property and the start date for the renovation.

Things were progressing smoothly. With a smile on my face and a cup of Cinnamon Plum Tea in hand, I was content with the progress for the tea room. Cinnamon Plum Tea is an herbal blend with currants, succulent hibiscus and hints of plum, accented with cinnamon and naturally sweet licorice root. It's warm and soothing, yet fruity and full bodied with a deep red infusion. Wonderful. Just what I needed to relax and contemplate the future.

Tuesday, I planned to drive to Metuchen to give deposit checks to all the contractors. Calling Stacy for lunch or dinner was my next order of business.

"Hi Stacy. I'll be in town tomorrow. Let's do lunch."

"I have a Zumba class at 10:00, but I'll be free anytime after 11:30."

"I'll pick you up at the "Y" noonish. I need to broaden my horizons in terms of local restaurants. Think of a new and interesting one."

I hadn't been to the 'Y" in years. Walking up the front step, I encountered a sign stating the front entrance was closed. I walked around to the back, discovering an entirely new and grand entrance. I walked inside to a large reception desk and waiting area, asking the receptionist to page Stacy.

"Hi Stacy, where are we going for lunch? I've already been to the Duchess Dinner, let's try another place. And what a change in this old 'Y', can't believe it."

"How about the Frenchie Love Café? It's a small coffee place. Thought you'd like to compare it to what you were thinking for the tea room," said Stacy.

It was not cheerful inside-- dark walls, dark floor, and dark tables.

Reading the menu, I said, "This is fairly standard with no frills-featuring hamburgers and fries, club sandwiches, a few salads and vegetable soup. As soup is my favorite, I'll order that with a small salad." Stacy had the same.

"Stacy, is your soup cold?"

"Yes" We sent the soup back. The salad was okay, nothing special. All in all, I figured the tea room would present a better appearance and menu. Score one for me and the Bonnie Neuk.

"I've been working on the menu for the tea room. There would be a soup special each day with my white bean and lime chicken soup as standard fare, accompanied by a mini quiche or several small sandwiches with a Mediterranean chickpea salad or broccoli salad. I'd like to offer a few sweets such as flavored scones, Devonshire cream, my great chocolate-chocolate cake, and maybe, periodically, a cheese cake."

"That all sounds wonderful. Can't wait until you're open. I'll taste anything out for you," she said with a giggle. "If you need to stay tonight, let me know"

"Thanks. I might take you up on that. I'll call you later."

My phone's ring startled me. *"Why don't you use the Scottish Shortbread cookie recipe that was handed down by your grandmother? I bet she used them in her tea room."* As always, the phone went dead. I looked at it with an angry face. Stacy glanced at me with a strange look as if to say 'what's wrong?'

"I keep getting these phone calls with ideas for the tea room."

"That's odd," Stacy said. "Perhaps it's someone playing a joke on you. Don't worry about it."

"Maybe, but some of these strange ideas have been helpful. Like this one about shortbread cookies to be used in the tea room." Finishing our lunch, I dropped Stacy back at the "Y" and drove to Ron's office.

"I applied for building permits and discussed plans with

Bran Randal and Chris Checks. He felt it would, indeed, be a good idea to contact the neighbor for extra parking. If you promise to pave the driveway and plow in the winter, as well as provide some financial compensation, he'll consider the idea. We'll have to go before the Board to obtain a variance, but it won't be difficult," stated Ron.

I called Perry to check on the preliminary plans and then drove to Hilliard McDonald's office to give him his deposit check and a set of plans. It was 4:00 when I arrived at Hilliard's office. His receptionist said he was with a client. While waiting for him to complete a previous appointment, I perused some of the landscape magazines on the end table. Some of the ideas were fascinating in terms of how they used color and texture to create warmth and patterns in a garden. More creative ideas for my small garden.

"Victoria, you can go into Mr. McDonald's office," the receptionist said as she motioned with her hand.

"Hello, Hilliard. I was looking through the magazines getting additional ideas. We have discussed the many items that I would like on the phone and I am sure you have been taking notes and are ready to go. Here is the deposit check. Hopefully we can start as soon as settlement is completed on April 15."

"If you'd like, take some of the magazines and look them over for new ideas. I want this garden to be a product of your thoughts, images and feelings as well as my insight and horticultural knowledge. Let's make it a team effort."

"That sounds great. I can give you some ideas of what I like in a garden. I love hostas. Any size, color and shape-they are my favorites. Second, are daylilies because they appear graceful and soft. And grasses-feather grass is another among my favorite. I'll take these two magazines and look through them over the next few days. Thanks."

"That's a wonderful start. We can incorporate your

favorites into the back garden and around the fountain. I like those choices. In fact, I would normally recommend them in a small garden such as yours," Hilliard explained. Taking a deep breath he asked "A new bistro has opened in town, the Novita Bistro and Lounge. It used to be the Corner Stone. Would you like to enjoy an early dinner with me?" Hilliard asked with an inviting smile.

I felt panicky. Not two in a row...but I had to think positively. Stop worrying, he appears to be a gentleman. Or maybe a wolf in sheep's clothing. "That would be great. I had been there when it was the Corner Stone. When did it become the Novita?"

"It seems to change the name and ownership every third year. Last time was a year ago. Give me a few minutes to wrap things up here at the office and we'll head out."

CHAPTER 12

"Bread and water can so easily be
toast and tea."
Author Unknown

We pulled into the parking lot of the Novitia Bistro and walked in. A jazz singer was about to perform. Needless to say, the tables and bar were crowded and the atmosphere electric. The featured singer was reputed to have the same sound as Norah Jones. She was singing *"Come Away with Me."* As we walked to our table, she slid into *"Creepin' In"*. She definitely sounded like Norah.

"I had a feeling it would be crowded. I made a reservation," Hilliard remarked.

"The atmosphere has changed since the last time I had lunch here," I said. I like someone who plans ahead.

Given a menu and asked for a drink order, I ordered my usual white wine and Hilliard, a sapphire gin on the rocks with a twist. Here we go again, but maybe I should just go with the flow. We talked about where he went to school—Penn State. I had gone to Trenton State, which is now The College of New Jersey. He'd been married for over twenty-five years before he divorced with three grown children now on their own, as I did. We talked about rising college costs, the bleak economy, unemployment rates, and life in general. He certainly had his head on straight and was not reticent in asking questions and giving honest answers. During one of the slow songs, he asked me to dance. There were several others couples on the dance floor enjoying the music. It was comfortable to be in someone's arms. I had missed dancing.

We talked as if we were old friends. Suddenly, it was after nine o'clock; I had to return to Pennsylvania—long drive ahead. I apologized, but explained that I really needed to get back. Arriving at his office, he walked me to my car. Opening the door, he took my hand and kissed it.

"Thank you for accompanying me to the new club. It was a fun night."

"Thanks for a lovely evening," I said. "The food was good, the singer excellent, but the company even better. I had a good time, Hilliard. I'll see you soon. You'll call me when you have the final plans?"

"My pleasure. They should take three to four days to complete. I have several good CAD operators who can put this together quickly. I'll call you and we can review them and make changes if need be. Keep me abreast of the closing date. I have a sub contractor with whom I have discussed the job. I want to keep him in the loop, so he's ready when you are. " Hilliard told me to drive carefully. I waved goodbye. It had been a comfortable and relaxing evening. Realizing that I would be living in this town put a smile on my face. Maybe next time I should stay at Stacy's during the week. It would make more sense.

CHAPTER 13

"You are going out for tea today, so mind how you behave. Let all accounts I hear of you, Be pleasant ones, I crave."
Kate Greenaway

The few weeks before settlement went like wildfire.

Liz had called with her basic findings on the research of the house. "Something more in depth would take time and money. The house is well over hundred years old and was originally built by the Van Dorr family, who lived there for more than fifty years. They were a family of six with four children—three boys and a girl. The three boys were all in the military, but two of them died while in service. The next owner was there for fifteen years—a young couple, Coopers. The last owner, Merriwithers, lived there for over forty years, a family of four with only the two children left alive. The parents both died in the house."

"Liz, will you email all the information to me? I'll

create a file and add these pages to it. Maybe soon I'll do the extensive search." It was interesting, but nothing out of the ordinary.

Settlement day was finally here. We met at the house for a final walk-through. The family's attorney was present since it was an estate sale. When we arrived at the third floor area in the bedroom section, the attorney leaned down and fiddled with a wire low to the floor. Suddenly a section of wall opened to disclose a small secret area in back of the bedroom.

The attorney explained, "This was a secret false closet that had been created when the house was built. There is a second secret closet located somewhere else, but the children of the owners didn't know where it was." The opening was from floor to ceiling—about one-foot deep and two-feet wide, with several shelves. It looked like it was used to store files.

"That's interesting. Any idea why they had it built?"

"It seems that the Mr. Van Dorr worked for a secret government agency and often took documents home to work on. It's interesting that there's a second hiding place," stated the attorney.

"I guess I have my work cut out for me to find the other area. Hopefully, I would."

Shortly after our walk-through, I found myself signing the deed, mortgage documents, and numerous other papers. We had to wait until the Wells Fargo mortgage check was wired into the previous owners' account. Everything else went smoothly and, two hours later, the house was mine. I was excited; the smile would not come off my face.

"Congratulations, Victoria, you're the proud owner of

what will become The Bonnie Neuk Tea Room," said Richard.

Even though I had had an unpleasant experience with him, he did work hard to help me obtain my dream house, starting me on the way to completing my tea room: The Bonnie Neuk named after my grandmother's tea room.

CHAPTER 14

"There is no trouble so great or grave that can not be much diminished by a nice cup of tea."
Bernard-Paul Heroux

Renovations started the next day and were well under-way during the first week. The fountain was scheduled to arrive in two weeks. The surrounding area was going to be planted around the spot for the fountain. Hilliard and I had discussed the plants, the appearance I wanted, and the views from the porch and the tables. It was turn-ing out even better than I had envisioned. We used my recommendations, plus several of Hilliard's ideas. The effect and ambiance was overwhelming—it looked peaceful and serene. New Jersey is cold in the late fall and winter, so I couldn't use the porch area with the view of the garden year round. It would be a warm weather experience from mid May to late September. Four to five tables will seat twenty to twenty four people. Perfect for small parties and meetings. The small room next to the kitchen would be used for meetings. Hilliard was stopping in later to discuss the upcoming week and plans for completion.

I was busy unpacking when one of the workmen yelled that the landscape architect was downstairs. I checked my appearance in the mirror and went to meet Hilliard.

"Hello, Victoria. How's the renovation progressing?" Hilliard inquired, as he looked around at the parking and the back porch area.

"There were a few snags that we dealt with, but we're doing well. I'll move into the third floor in a few weeks. It'll make it easier to oversee the renovations. How do you think the garden looks?"

"We've accomplished a lot in the last week. The stone edging will make the meeting of the garden and the paths look neat and keep the dirt away from the paths. I like the effect. The porch, garden, and canopy area will be finished in the next two weeks," he said enthusiastically. He was the driving force, making sure this was all completed on schedule.

"It looks super. I'm pleased." We chatted about the progress and what was going to happen next week. I suggested seasonal flowers, orchids, and small trees to soften the area.

"I'd love orchids hanging off the canopy. Although not able to stay permanently, I feel they'd add a great deal to the overall appearance. My favorite is the ghost orchid. I have several, as well as brighter orchids in storage at my children's places. What are your thoughts?"

"They definitely add atmosphere and color. Bring them next time and we'll plant them in fancy hanging pots. During the winter months, you can hang them in the windows inside."

"I have more work to do at the office, but I was wondering if you'd like to try out the new Country Western Bar and Grill in Edison. I haven't heard good or bad about it, but it'll be a fun time. I'll be finished in a few hours." Hilliard said with a hopeful smile.

"Sounds great. I enjoy country western music. Is there dancing, too?" I asked.

"I don't know, but it wouldn't surprise me. I'll call, make a reservation and ask. Did you want me to call you back about the dancing?"

"No, that won't be necessary. I'm sure it will be enjoyable with or without a little dance music. We'll give it a try." Wonderful, this would be my second date with Hilliard. I'd planned to stay over tonight at Stacy's. Good thing.

"I'll pick you up in two hours." As he got into his car, his hand touched mine. Wow, what an electric current.

I wasn't sure what to wear to a country western bar. I tried on my skinny jeans and realized I could lose a few pounds. I'm resigning from the 'clean plate club,' Dad," I said out loud. He was the originator and president of the club. It used to be his favorite saying. "Eat everything on your plate and you can be a member of the 'clean plate club.' But if I want my skinny jeans to fit better, I'll need to quit. Sorry, Dad.

I was nervous, but not sure why. I ran down the stairs to answer the doorbell and head out for our second date.

The western bar was great and had music. We danced a few line sets and some heel n' toe moves. The food was quite good, but I really didn't notice much except Hilliard.

It wasn't late when Hilliard brought me back to the tea room. We talked about the fun we had dancing and laughed about missing steps. He gently took me into his arms and kissed me. It started as a soft kiss, but quickly changed into something intense. The man could kiss. I parted my lips. His tongue and mine met. I was getting all warm and tingly. We stood on the back porch inter-

twined in each others arms. It felt right.

I came up for air and said, "Thanks for a great time. I need to work on those line dances, but it was an experience. I have to ask you something."

"What?"

"When you kissed me, was that a 'lets-have dinner-again sometime' kiss, or was it something more? Was it more like I'd like to see you soon and start something?"

"It more I'd like to see you soon and maybe start something. You'll be living here and it will be easier to go out. I had a good time too. When are you moving into the tea room? You have a long drive tonight."

"I'm moving to the third floor in two weeks. Waiting on a few cabinets and several doors. I was planning to stay at Stacy's tonight since I didn't want to make that long drive."

"That's smart. It'll be nice to have you close-by. I'll call in a few days. There are things to complete on the garden, as well as installing the fountain. See you soon." He squeezed my hand and headed for his car.

"Good night." Victoria, don't rush things. Take it slow… remember you just got out of a twenty-five-year marriage.

Second floor bedrooms and third floor efficiency were shaping up. The contractor had two teams working on the property. I met Ron on the second floor. "How do you think everything is coming along?"

"I have one team working on the second and third floors. My second team is working in the tea room area and kitchen with a subcontractor doing the plumbing in the kitchen. I remember you had considered eventually making the second floor bedrooms into a bed and breakfast. Sounds interesting," said Ron.

"The studio apartment on the third floor is turning

out just how I had envisioned it. One large room with a small area for a kitchen and bathroom. You have most of the kitchen cabinets replaced and the new appliances installed. Just need to upgrade the bathroom a bit to make it bright and cheery," I said.

"It should be completed within the week."

"Great, I'm looking forward to that. I'll move here as soon as it is completed."

One of the workmen looked into the room seemingly annoyed. "I know this sounds crazy, but I can't find my lunch bag. Have either of you seen it in your travels around the house this morning?"

"No, Vincent, where did you last see it?" asked Ron.

"I could have sworn I'd put it on the mantel in the living room."

"One of the guys must be pulling a prank on you," Ron said. "Why don't you ask the workers in the kitchen area?"

Vincent walked down the stairs and yelled. "Hey guys, have you seen my lunch bag? Did you hide it on me?"

Another worker said, "You most likely ate it already and forgot."

"It's not like someone took it or it floated away." Another worker checked the kitchen, the mud room, and finally the small bathroom. There on the back of the toilet tank was the lunch bag.

"Who did that?" the worker asked.

"Not me," answered one of the other workmen.

"None of us did." And they all laughed and went back to work.

"We will start work on the garage apartment in five weeks," said Ron.

"Once that is completed, it will be my new home. I'm looking forward to a new color scheme . Good riddance to the olive green appliances." We both laughed, remembering the awkward moment about the green stuff.

The light cherry kitchen cabinets with granite counter top featuring light apricot tones will blend well with the cabinets. The small counter area will serve as a table with room for two or three stools. I would like numerous new windows installed in the back area, adding to the brightness of the kitchen, as well as a small balcony on the side of the kitchen with stairs leading down to the outside. This way I could have several chairs and an end table on the balcony to enjoy the gardens and fountain. There will be a new partition to create a master bedroom and small spare bedroom. My desk and files will fit perfectly at the end of the master bedroom.

"Ron, I have purchased shelves for the garage to store boxes until there is time to unpack things." As soon as I move into the third floor apartment, I would begin work on the marketing plan for the tea room. Lots of work to do, I was up for it.

The contractors were working on the gift store area, creating nooks and cubby holes to make the area friendly and comfortable. The kitchen and pantry areas were turning out to be more spacious than expected and included places for the tins of tea. The back porch required more thought despite my expectations of a lovely garden and fountain.

While the contractors worked on the house, I'd work on the business plan for the tea room. My phone rang and I noted the caller ID, "Hi, Tammy."

"What are you doing? Maybe we could do a quick lunch?" she asked.

"Sounds like a great idea. I'll meet you at the Inn in fifteen minutes."

I walked across the street and found a table for us. It felt good to sit and relax. I waved as Tammy came in. "Over here." She sat down, we checked the menu and ordered.

"What have you been doing with yourself the last few

weeks? I've missed you"

"Keeping my nose to the grindstone. To publicize the Bonnie Neuk, I interviewed with the *Metuchen Recorder*, the *Edison Sentinel*, and *The Home News*. I joined the Chamber of Commerce to take part in community events. Getting my name out there is the name of the game. I'm advertising on some local placemats and promotional discount booklets."

"Sounds like you've been very busy. It keeps you out of trouble."

"Busy, but having fun. Put my website online, www.thebonnieneuktearoom.com, whose motto is "Come back often to the Bonnie Neuk where there is always something new 'a brewing.' " "

"That's unique. I like it!" Tammy laughed.

"I also set up an email account at: thebonnieneuktearoom@gmail.com. People in town and the surrounding areas can check out what we're offering, be aware of our grand opening and email me if they have questions. The size and color of the signage in front of the tea room was stipulated by the Metuchen Board. Contacting the BIL (The Borough Improvement League) and the Red Hat Society, I was able to book special events in advance. Several church groups reserved space for their afternoon meetings. Since the tea room is near the Borough Hall and several office complexes, my thought is they might periodically come for lunch. I went into each facility, talked to the person in charge, gave them flyers to post, and explained the basics of the tea room. Then I contacted organizations and stores, left flyers, and chatted with them. I also designed laminated menus to distribute."

"Your feet are on the ground ready to walk; no, you're ready to run."

"Yes, it's all coming together. Maybe tomorrow you could come over for lunch. I'd like your opinion on the

menu. A second pair of eyes is always good."

"Sounds like a plan. I'll be over around 1:00. Make sure some of your infamous White Bean and Lime Chicken soup is available."

"Will do!"

CHAPTER 15

"All you're supposed to do is every once in a while give the boys a little tea and sympathy."
Robert Anderson

It had been a whirlwind few weeks, beginning with arrangements with a mover to pick up my possessions in Pennsylvania and deliver them to my new home in Metuchen. Sounded easy, but took forever. Had enough furniture to fill every bedroom on the second and third floor, eventually, the garage apartment. The movers set up everything in the places I indicated. Many of the boxes will end up on the garage shelves. Things will be sorted later, and then I'll begin searching for new items.

Aunt Jane's barrel chair went in the corner of the third floor bedroom where I'd sit to read, relax, and think. I'm a great believer in angels for love and protection. I hung several mobiles featuring these celestial beauties near the barrel chair, my way of making this my home; one

in the bedroom to catch the morning light and another in the kitchen to protect and bless.

Working hard until late in the evening, I wanted to unwind. The best way is to make a cup of Rooibos tea and relax in Auntie's chair that enveloped me with its sturdy arm. It made me feel secure. These herbal leaves or tisanes are from Africa. Tisane is a catch-all term for any non-caffeinated beverage made from the infusion of herbs and/or spices. It is naturally caffeine free with a rich red color and a sweet nutty flavor.

Closing my eyes to inhale the fragrance of the nutty tea, I felt a cool breeze and a hint of lavender. Suddenly, the room became extremely cold and the hairs on the back of my neck stood up. Despite my fear, I looked up to see in the far corner of the room what looked like a person—a young man, his body image not defined, but rather fuzzy. I stared at the figure until I gathered enough courage to speak. "I pray for the white light to protect me. My name is Victoria Thorn Storm. Having bought this house as a means to a new start for my life, I mean you no harm and come in peace. My dream is to remodel this house into The Bonnie Neuk, a tea room similar to the one my grandmother Thorn had in Metuchen many years ago. Who are you? What is your name? What do you want?" The room remained deadly cold and quiet. His shape became more defined, and I noticed he was dressed in a WWII Army uniform. I sat still for what seemed like hours. In reality only minutes had passed.

The voice said with surprise, "You can see me? Time is irrelevant. I have been drifting in this house for many years. I can't leave. Most people don't see or hear me, and some have tried to ignore me. I want to be known and looked upon with respect. I am a soldier and have fought for the honor of my country. I was one of the twenty-seven killed many years ago in a freak bus and train accident. We were returning to the base from maneuvers.

I was the oldest soldier. The young man sitting next to me was twenty one. Your name sounds familiar. Did I know you? My name is Derrick," he stated in a scratchy, but audible voice. "I hope to be friends with the owner of this house."

On a hunch, I asked him, "Did you move a lunch bag the other day?"

"I could have... It did make everyone laugh." After a long pause he said, "I will return."

The air turned warmer and the room silent. The voice, fuzzy figure, and the smell of lavender vanished as quickly as they had appeared. It's unnerving from the get-go to realize that you are seeing a ghost, let alone talking to one. I really need to understand what was going on and why I was able to communicate with this ghost. My nerves were a little jangled to say the least.

I should ask Liz to investigate more of the history of the past owners of this house. I had to tell her about my experience with the ghost of the soldier. Not that she would believe it. I own a house, complete with a soldier's ghost, and someone who keeps calling my cell phone. Could there be a connection? How lucky am I? Maybe I'm going crazy.

Remembering Tammy's conversation awhile back about the application for ghost finding on the iPhone, maybe it was time to really consider a smart phone. Mine was still dumb. Would it stop the anonymous phone calls? Think I'll call Tammy.

"Tammy, you mentioned the ghost finder on your IPhone. How do you communicate with the spirit world? And what is electronic voice phenomenon (EVP)?"

"Communicating with the beyond can be costly and time-intensive. You could bypass the séance route and find someone who studied EVP (the practice of looking for hidden voices in recorded white noise) or perhaps a follower of Thomas Edison, who was thought to have

worked on a 'spirit phone' or psychic phone during his lifetime. Ghosts are extremely sensitive; they can pick up on our thoughts and feelings with crystal-clear clarity, as if they possessed some kind of special radar. Ghosts are "stuck" souls that are either "in the light" or "earth-bound." They want to communicate with us, not scare us. No one can set them free unless we show them the light. There is a tunnel where many of our deceased loved ones are waiting for us on the other side. The end of the tunnel, which is the entrance to the other side, is a brilliant white light. Souls call this 'Home'; we call it heaven. They remain on earth for various reasons. Many don't know they are dead or want to make sure their loved ones are safe. They feel guilty leaving their loved ones without warning. Some feel they are too young to die, or there is still work to be done on earth, or are not yet ready to leave earth. Energy doesn't die. Among the living some people can communicate with ghosts, most can't. I guess you're one of the lucky ones, you can."

"Wow, that is so-o enlightening. You really have knowledge on ghosts. My ghost wants to be friends and lives in my tea room. He says there are others that come and go. Great! Thanks for all the knowledge, Tammy. We'll talk tomorrow."

"You have a ghost. How cool. You'll have to tell me more when I see you."

The next morning I called Liz to see if she could find more information about the former owners. Even it there was a charge, I'd like to know more.

"Hi, Victoria. I did check in-depth and discovered a few additional things. I'm not sure I believe them or if you'll want to hear about them," Liz said hesitantly.

Before she could say anything else, I said, "I know you

are not a believer, but I had a strange first night in the house. This sixth sense, or psychic ability, is known as intuition, gut feeling, a hunch, or a certain knowingness. We all use this ability often subconsciously. For instance, how many times have you thought of someone, and minutes later the phone rings and that person is on the other end. Or you have a hunch to switch routes home and you find out later there was a bad accident along your usual route. Have you ever had that experience? Perhaps you had a feeling on the way to work that the boss was in a tizzy. And sure enough she was. How many times have you been thinking of a song, and minutes later you hear it on the radio? These are some of the psychic things that have happened to me. We all have psychic ability, but some are greater than others."

"I think I've had a few experiences like that, but I'm not sure what I'd call it or whether I believe it," Liz replied.

"Anyway, what did you find out about the house? Then I'll tell you what happened last night."

"You certainly have peaked my curiosity. Some of this I already mentioned. The house had three owners: Van Dorr, Coopers, and Merriwither. It was built in the early 1900. One of the Van Dorr sons was killed in a freak accident when he was on his way to ship out during World War II. One son was named Daniel, the other was named Derrick." My eyes popped and my mouth dropped. I stopped breathing for a minute and looked at the phone in amazement.

"Some say he haunts the house. Several people have reported hearing something. I'm sure they're imagining things."

"Well, Liz, I saw a young man in a military uniform last night. He said his name was Derrick and I think he was a ghost. I felt a cold breeze on my neck just before the room got frigid. The outline of the young man was fuzzy at first and, how do I say this, his edges weren't

defined. He was transparent. He gave me his name and said he'd be back."

"That's scary. You're making me wonder if I should rethink this ghost thing. No, no, it's hard for me to believe there are ghosts. No, I'm sure there are no such things as ghosts. Aren't you a little freaked out? It's giving me goosebumps."

She thinks I'm crazy. Maybe I am. "I was definitely freaked out, but I think he comes in peace and doesn't mean any harm. The experience was unnerving!"

"Do you know what he wants? Should I stay at your house tonight. No, I don't want to do that. Maybe you come to mine? Just in case…" I'm sure Liz didn't completely believe my experience, but she was concerned for me as her friend. "I don't like you there alone, but I'm not sure I'd like to experience the fuzzy- edged soldier, either."

"I'll be fine, but I'll keep my phone nearby just in case. I've heard it said that to understand the living, you've got to communicate with the dead. I think I'm doing that." There was a strange feeling in the pit of my stomach. "I was certainly communicating with some entity last night. Meet Derrick, the ghost."

The next night went smoothly, no visitors or strange events. I was able to have a good night's sleep and planned to do some garage sale and thrift store shopping the next day. I had lots of items that were needed to make the tea room look vintage. Love garage sales and discovering bargains. Would my ghost be pleased that I'm shopping for used linens, tea cups, and tables for the tea room? Why should I care if he is pleased? Am I nuts?

CHAPTER 16

"The path to heaven passes through a teapot."
Ancient Proverb

Early the next morning, I checked the local paper and earmarked five garage sales around Metuchen and one estate sale in Perth Amboy. Then I'll try the local thrift stores, Goodwill, and various consignment shops. I'd avoided pricey antique stores or paying top dollar. How had my grandmother furnished her tea room in 1932? Did they have garage sales or consignment shops in those days?

The cell phone interrupted my thoughts. *"Ask friends and family to clean out their closets and give you all the mismatched china, linens, chairs, tables, and other items they no longer need. The response from friends could be great. You'll get plenty of things and then some. Try that."* The phone went dead. Who keeps calling me? I checked the phone for a number. Again it said "no data." Unnerving to say the least.

Setting out at 6:30 AM, I wanted to arrive early at the first sale. It was going to be an adventurous day. I loved the idea of discovering a special bargain at a good price. I'd stowed a bunch of towels in the back of my 'schlepping,' roomy SUV and included several cardboard boxes. The Bonnie Neuk needed to feature unusual vintage items. Mix and match was the order of the day. Tea always tastes better in an old china cup, never a mug. My phone rang again. *"Holding a cup and saucer makes one sit up straight!"*

"Who is …." As always, no one was there. These phone calls continue to puzzle me. What is going on? I need to investigate this more and call the phone company again.

My search centered on china and silverware, chairs, and tables. I was looking for some hand-embroidered, trimmed, lace table linens. Linen napkins were not practical. Disposable paper ones would be a saving grace, because ironing was not my thing. I wasn't thinking of the environment. Sorry. Each table would have either a small vase or a tiny glass with flowers. The farthest sale was in Perth Amboy, so I headed there first, then, back to town. Maybe I'd get lucky at the estate sale.

Arriving at the estate sale early, I was confronted with a lovely old home with lots of character. And maybe a few ghosts? My hopes were high, but after wandering through each room, nothing caught my eye. I asked the homeowner if she had china, linens, or silverware.

"No, I'm sorry. We don't have many small items. Three beds, a dining room set, a few chairs, and items in the rooms off the kitchen." She showed me the way to the back.

In the far corner was a small, neglected, wooden table, which appeared to have been painted. I knew it could be refinished and covered with a linen cloth. The homeowner lowered the asking price to $25.00. "It needs a lot of love."

"I'll take it. You're right. I have to put some elbow grease and lots of love into it." She helped me carry it to my SUV. Great price, great find.

Driving back toward Metuchen, I stopped at several additional garage sales. The first one had nothing much of interest except several wide brimmed hats that caught my eye. My plan was to have a wall in the tea room displaying vintage hats, gloves, and jewelry. Guests could choose something from "The Wall" to wear during their dining experience.

Two more garage sales had been picked over by earlier customers, but at the third I found a marvelous antique Gibson luster and royal blue tea pot with matching sugar and creamer of English origin. Paying $50.00 for both seemed like a steal. It would be displayed on a shelf in the tea room. I already had a collection of teapots from my grandmothers and mother (she loved luster). At the fourth sale, I was able to pick up a nice white teapot and some odd plates.

There was at least a month before the tea room would be ready. When should I open? Was there a special day? My phone rang. *"I suggested before that you open the tea room on your mother's birthday, August 9. It would be a lovely way to honor her."*

"Who is this," but once again, a hang up. I must take my phone to be checked at Verizon. It was beginning to freak me out that it would ring, state something of current interest, and the line would go dead.

I had trouble locating the last garage sale; my GPS came to the rescue. Ahead, an old, worn-out house came into view. However, once inside, I couldn't believe my eyes. On the table was a grouping of china displayed with a sign that read, "Set of twelve." This was "the crème de la crème," an entire set! Immediately I identified it as

English bone china. The white cups were adorned with a few flowers; the saucers and plates had the same royal blue band. Beautiful. The set included dessert, luncheon, and dinner plates, as well as a tea pot, sugar and creamer, and several serving platters. Expecting an outrageous price, I asked, "What is the cost of this china set?"

"This was my grandmother's set. She brought it from England many years ago. Before she died, she gave it to me. I'm selling her house and have no room for them in the apartment I'm renting in Edison. I'm moving there in a few weeks to start summer school. I hate to give it up, but I must move on."

"Let me know the cost of the set?"

"Two hundred dollars," explained the young woman with a nostalgic expression on her face.

"I'll take it. It's lovely. I'll treasure it. What's your name and where in Edison are you moving?"

"Samantha Cummings, but friends call me Sam. I'm moving a few miles down the road and will begin taking summer classes at Middlesex Community College in a few weeks. Then more classes in early fall. I haven't decided if I am going to day or night classes."

"Well, Sam. Here's a promise. I'm opening a tea room in Metuchen in the next three months. You can visit anytime you like to see your grandmother's tea set." Her face glowed.

"She would enjoy the idea that someone is putting her china to good use. I'll indeed visit your tea room. What's the name and address of your place?"

"My name is Victoria Storm, and it will be The Bonnie Neuk Tea Room." I gave her one of my new business cards. "Your grandmother's tea set will be a welcome addition to my collection of teapots on display."

It was late in the afternoon when I returned with all my "goodies". Although enjoyable, it was a busy and tiring day. I needed something to pick me up. Searching my new tea recipes for something different, I picked a Turmeric tea.

Turmeric is the spice used in Indian curry to both color the food a yellowish shade and add to the taste. It's also used in mustard condiments for color. It has healing properties; anti-inflammatory to help to detox the body and also reduces pain. Not bad for one cup of tea. The turmeric has a distinct earthy, slightly bitter, hot peppery flavor and a mustardy smell. I used a cup of almond soy milk, which I heated then whisked in a half teaspoon of turmeric, one quarter teaspoon of ginger, and added a little honey to sweeten. It's a comforting drink. Sitting in the chair and sipping this peppery flavored turmeric, I felt the air grow cool, then cold. I looked up quickly and saw the soldier, Derrick, standing close by. He was fuzzy at the edges. I wasn't comfortable with this, but I wasn't as frightened as I had been the first time. He didn't say anything, but merely stood there looking at me with what seemed like a grin.

Then he said , "Can you see me, Victoria?" in a slow, low voice. He was looking straight at me.

I hesitated for a minute, then answered, "Yes, Derrick, I can see you." But truth be known, I wasn't sure I wanted to see him or knew what to do now that I did.

"People say "I'd like to be a fly on the wall"; well I am able to be that fly. I have been watching you create your tea room from my old house. You have been putting your own feelings and taste into this house. If you need help, I am here. I can't leave the property.

"What do you mean you can't leave the property. Have you tried more than once."

"Maybe."

"What do you mean, maybe." I asked.

"I don't have all the answers." he hesitated then continued talking. "It looks cozy, and I think it will attract many town customers. Keep up the great work." He again smiled and faded into the air of the room, then disappeared from view.

That was weird! He appears out of the blue for no reason. He compliments me on my tea room and then vanishes. Maybe I'm hallucinating. No, I know I saw and spoke to him. I think I should do some Internet searches on ghosts. I need to figure out why he's making himself visible to me. I feel this is more than the fact he is stuck here and likes my improvements. Hmmm. He could be a wealth of knowledge about the house's past. Maybe I should cultivate this friendship. Should I have offered him tea? Crazy idea!

CHAPTER 17

"It snowed last year too: I made a snowman
and my brother knocked it down and I knocked
my brother down
and then we had tea."
Dylan Thomas "A Child's Christmas in Wales"

Since moving in, each day I could see improvements. Things were progressing well. The house should be finished in early July, the garage apartment in late August. I planned to have a "Complimentary Come in and Taste" before the grand opening mid August.

I had bought myself a smart phone, which was still a mystery, and a landline for the Bonnie Neuk. The landline startled me when it rang. It was Stacy.

"Hi, Victoria, how are things progressing? I'm sure you're busy."

"You're correct. Kinda over my head busy. I've spent a lot of time researching tea distributors, as well as methods of ordering teas and checking prices. I have made charts with prices, types of tea, delivery times, and eventually decided on two distributors who are reliable and reasonable—Rishi Tea and Tea Fonte. Some of my ideas for the gift shop are selling tea sets, fancy spoons, recipes and other books such as Jan Whitaker's *Tea at the Blue Lantern Inn*, also a variety of teas and honey."

"I'm free for an hour or so. How about lunch? You can tell me what's happening with all your new projects."

"Sounds great. Come over and try my mini-quiche. I can use your opinion."

"Be there in twenty."

I had a few minutes to spare to look for my notebook. I know I had put it down on my desk a few hours ago, but I can't find it. Guess I'm getting older than I think. I'm misplacing things more often. Or maybe I'm so busy, I'm not remembering.

When Stacy arrived, I immediately put her to work heating soup, while I assembled goat cheese and water cress sandwiches and a sample of the mini-quiche.

"Tell me what you've been checking and researching the last week. You're always a wealth of information and knowledge," said Stacy.

"I've been doing research on honey and learned more on the subject of bees. According to the National Honey Board, there are more than three hundred unique types of flavors available in the U.S. Honey has a flavor distinctive to a particular plant. Bees make honey from the nectar they carry from flowers, trees, and plants.

"I thought they added flavors once the honey was harvested and ready to package. That's so cool!"

"Did you know that to obtain an apple flavored honey, the growers put the beehives right in the middle of an apple orchard? Some other examples are melon flavor, goldenrod, and dandelion which adds a strong taste to honey. I love using honey in my teas, as well as cooking with it. Nothing like butter and honey on an apple or cranberry scone. But my personal favorite is lavender honey. You heat the honey and add several lavender blossoms. It adds a wonderful flavor to your tea or scone."

"You've done a great job researching. I'll have to try the lavender honey. What else has been on the checking-out list?"

"I'm also researching smoothies. They're all the rage, you know. I want to serve one or two different types for occasional specials. It's frozen yogurt with ice cubes made of teas. You can use green tea cubes with a cup of fruit such as strawberries, blueberries, or melon, or make a peach Rooibos smoothie using honey. They're all good tasting. I want to offer my guests Biscotti also. I checked into several distributors but settled for the one in Bucks County, Pennsylvania. It had a good selection and offered wholesale prices."

"Everything sounds great and I'm sure it'll be a hit." said Stacy. "How about dinner with 'the ladies' on Thursday night at the Inn? We haven't seen much of you lately. I'll give everyone a call."

"Sounds great. Why don't you have them come here first? I'd love to have opinions on things featured in the gift shop. I've collected names and email addresses to create a database of clients. Before my grand opening, I want to email a flyer to announce the grand opening. I placed an ad in the local papers requesting kitchen help, waitress and waiters, pastry chef, and assistants. I've already had several people for a tasting event and a special tea party for someone's daughter. I'll need an accountant to help with the financial end of the business. Any suggestions of someone who might be good? I guess one thing at a time."

"Let me do some thinking on the accountant. Maybe ask Liz, she might have a good suggestion."

"Stacy, I see the contractor coming in. I need to talk with him for a minute. I'll be right back. Help yourself to more soup." I walked into the tea room to catch up with Ron.

"I've been meaning to talk to you. Have you or your workers found anything that resembles a small secret area or hiding place?"

"What do you mean?"

"When I bought the house, the attorney for the estate showed me a secret closet on the third floor. He said there was another one somewhere else in the house, but didn't know where."

"I'm sure my workers would have said something, but I'll ask them. We'll keep our eyes open. The only place we haven't done extensive renovations is in the basement. That's piled up with wood for the porch, cabinets and windows for the apartment. I'll mention it to my workers and let you know."

"Thanks so much." I returned to the kitchen. Stacy and I chatted about dinner, and I was telling her about additional things I was considering for the gift store.

"The quiche was great and I love the soup. I need to stop eating and get back to work. See you later."

Ron stuck his head in the kitchen, "Oh, by the way, I found your notebook in the back bathroom." He handed it to me.

"Don't know how it got there. But thanks." I scratched my head. I wonder if it is my ghost? Listen to me, my ghost!

There were ten messages on my cell phone. Each was in reference to the jobs. While checking my messages, another call came in. I waited with anticipation to hear who was calling.

"Hello, Victoria. This is Sam. We met at a garage sale several weeks ago." I went quiet, I had to think. What garage sale? I think she could sense I was having difficulty placing her. She added, "You bought my grandmother's tea set."

"Oh, yes, Sam. How are you? I'm glad you called. I'll be putting the set on display shortly. We'll be opening the tea room in a few weeks."

"I was calling to answer your ad for a pastry chef. I am taking evening classes for pastry and cooking. I'd love to be a part of the Bonnie Neuk experience. I have numerous recipes from my grandmother, including scones, tarts, and a few quiches. Baking during the day and going to school at night works for me," Sam suggested.

"Why don't you come by, fill out an application, and we'll chat? Some of your grandmother's recipes would be helpful. I have a few also."

Another call clicked in and I asked Sam to come by the house later in the afternoon. The voice said. *"I mentioned before, why don't you have your grand opening on your mother's birthday, August 9?"* As always, the line went dead, but it sounded like a good date to strive for. And who was that on the line? Damn, this was my new phone. I looked at my phone like it had the plague. I stuck my tongue out at it. How childish? I didn't have time to deal with this now.

Six appointments were set up for waitresses and one kitchen helper the next day. I figured I'd make the soups myself each day, but I needed waitresses for the tables and someone to put the sandwiches together and help with making tea and plating the food.

Sam arrived at 3:00. She looked more relaxed than she had at her garage sale, more in charge and together. I showed her around the tea room and the kitchen with all its new stainless steel counters and sinks. We sat down to discuss what she was looking for and what I needed. She could work five days a week from 8 to 3 and, if there were special events, we could work around them. The large double freezer and refrigerator would allow things to be prepared ahead and stored. There was no question that I would hire her. It's uncanny how we met. Things do happen for a reason. I was working on putting together the Tea 101 lecture that I would give a few days before opening.

Over the next three days, I interviewed twelve people. I was able to hire a young woman, Lynda, who would help in the kitchen several days a week. Peter wanted to work three days during the week, some Saturdays and maybe special events. There were several women who wanted to waitress during the week and a high school student who could work on Saturdays for special parties. My kids were all pitching in too. Adam was going to help set up the gift shop and Ann and Frank were coming for a long weekend opening week; Anthony would be here for the third and fourth weekends. I was pretty well covered. Numerous things in boxes had to be unwrapped and put on the shelves in the gift shop for display. "Complimentary Come In and Taste" was planned for a few days before opening. Everything would be served in small amounts, but complimentary. Hopefully this would entice people to come back to sample the teas and food when we opened.

Having worked hard for the last three days, I needed some down time to unwind. Tea was my answer. I chose a decaffeinated peach tea. It was a Ceylon black flavored with ripe summer peaches with a sweet, syrup peach fragrance, lingering floral aromas as you sip the first as well as the middle and last taste.

A breeze stirred and it was almost as if I felt a gentle, soft touch…I breathed deeply and looked around the room. There was no one there. But yet, I could feel something.

"Who are you?" I asked, feeling someone was touching me.

"It's Derrick again. I need your help."

"Do normal people see ghosts?" I asked.

"Define normal."

I walked to the other side of the room. He followed. I could feel him. He tapped me on the shoulder. "Go away," I said with determination.

"I can't. You have a gift. You can hear and see me. Most cannot."

"Well, I don't want to… I don't want to see or talk to ghosts."

"I need your help. It's a gift talking to the dead," said Derrick.

"It's not a gift, it's damn scary."

We both sat there waiting for the other to speak. I took the lead trying to make small talk. "Does it feel warm in here?"

"I'm a ghost. I don't feel."

Small talk didn't work so I just said, "You said you wanted my help. What is it you need?"

"I worked with two friends a long time ago. It was a project…an apparatus or better yet, a machine. It was to be an invention. I've lost track of my friends and the invention. I wanted to reunite, but I can't find them. I need you to do some research. See if you can locate them or at least their families and see what happened to the project."

"Do you think they're alive? Why can't you check it out? Don't you have a 'Google Ghost' app?"

"You're funny. They're dead, I am sure. To the best of my ability, we can communicate with other souls. But I can't leave the property. I don't know why because the other ghosts living here can come and go as they choose. It is done all through thoughts and mental communication…no Google Ghost application that I know of."

"Derrick, how many other ghosts are living here?"

"There are three or four others; they come and go at different times."

"Oh great! My tea room not only has one ghost, but at least four. It's getting crowded. I guess I can try to find something for you. These next few weeks are going to be hectic, but after that I'll see what I could do. What are their names? And where did they live? Would their

families know about the machine?" I asked.

"We worked at the Edison Lab in Menlo Park. My friends and I were assistants. Sam Compton and Arnold Stump. I'm not sure where they lived, but I know it was in the Menlo Park—Metuchen area. Please see what you can do. There's no hurry, I've waited this long."

Derrick vanished, leaving me wondering what I would do with a house full of ghosts and how I was going to try to help him find his friends. Maybe I should run a haunted tea room—The Haunted Bonnie Neuk Tea Room. No, I don't think that would encourage customers. Or maybe it would?

CHAPTER 18

*"Good love affairs start with champagne and
end with tea."*
Author unknown

I wanted my employees to understand tea—how it is
grown, where it is grown, the different types of teas, their
tastes, and steeping times, so I prepared a crash course.
Passing out a small folder with this information, I started
with the history of tea: the Chinese Emperor, and how
the popularity of the beverage spread throughout China,
Asia, England, and eventually to the colonies.

"There are five types of teas with several additional
considerations. There is Black Tea, White Tea, Oolong
Tea, Green Tea, and herbal teas that encompass Rooibos
and pur-ee tea." I discussed their unique flavors and their
individual steeping times. "There are many websites
online. Spend a little time and Google them and learn
more about tea on your own."

"Victoria, you are saying there are different steeping times for the various teas?" asked Eleana, one of the waitresses.

"Yes, that's right there are. I enclosed a chart in your folder. It is set up in minutes.

> Green Tea 2-3 minutes
> White Tea 2-3 minutes
> Oolong Tea 3-4 minutes
> Black Tea 3-5 minutes
> Herbal 4-5 minutes."

"But why can't you steep each for two minutes and let it go at that?" questioned Eleana.

"Some teas turn bitter when steeped too long, and others need more time to obtain the rich flavor from the leaves," I explained. "If you want stronger tea, use more tea leaves, not more time steeping. This rule is written in stone."

"That makes sense. I do like my black tea strong and my green tea on the mild side," said Eleana.

We discussed iced tea and I showed them the two new decorative ice tea dispensers and neat-looking glasses. Everyone ooohed and aaahed.

"We'll have a standard soup each day, my white bean and lime chicken, plus a special soup. Lemongrass soup is another of my favorites. I'll put them on a board in front for customers to view as they walk in. If you have any special soups and recipes, please let me know and I'll consider them for our specials. We will also serve petite tea sandwiches. Does anyone know how the sandwich started?"

"I would guess some Mr. Sandwich put his name on two pieces of bread," replied Eleana.

"That's close. It is thought that the 4th Earl of Sandwich had inadvertently invented the British snack in the mid 18th century. He was at a gaming table and asked for some cold meat. So as to avoid greasy hands, he asked it to be served between two pieces of bread. Other gentleman at the table followed his lead and asked for 'the same as Sandwich!' The sandwich became incorporated into this 'new craze' of afternoon tea. It was eventually refined to a more elegant, bite size, sometimes crust free snack with tasty fillings. Hence the tea sandwich. This might be interesting to tell guests at the tea room."

"I want this to be a united effort. Sam will be making a variety of fresh scones each day. The cranberry pecans, blueberry, and chocolate chip will be our standard, but we'll have others, such as cinnamon pecan, blackberry, and a Chai spiced selection as specials. We'll serve tea sandwiches of egg salad, cucumber, chicken salad, and goat cheese with watercress, to name a few. I have enclosed a copy of the menu in each of your folders. Please check it out. I'm open to suggestions."

"I didn't know there was so much to making teas and serving. This is great," commented Lynda, another waitress. "It's like a Tea 101 course."

"Yes, in a way. But tea cannot be learned from a book or a course; it can only be learned from the heart. I want us all to be friends. There'll be times, at least I hope, when we're busy. I want us to work together for the satisfaction of the customer. That's it for now. Any questions?"

"Just one. When can we sample some of the wonderful sounding tea and scones? You know it's always better to recommend something you've already tasted," remarked Eleana with a mischievous grin.

"I get your drift. We can finish with class and enjoy some tasting and sampling. Sam's whipped up a batch of her great cranberry pecan scones." As I was saying this, Sam came out of the kitchen with a huge tray. I went back to bring out six steaming pots full of different teas and arranged them on the table. Each had a different appearance, and each contained a different hot and fragment tea. Time to enjoy a regular tea tasting party with my new worker bees.

CHAPTER 19

"Women are like tea bags, they don't know how strong they are until they get into hot water."
Eleanor Roosevelt

The house was being prepared for the grand opening. The workers were going back and forth putting things in place, repairing, mending, or adding to. My phone rang.

"Hi Victoria, it's Hilliard. I know you're very busy, but I wanted to wish you the best with your tasting event and your grand opening. I'll try to get over to sample some. But let's plan to go to dinner next week when things settle down a little."

"Next week will be great. I should have things under control by then and will need a break. Several teams are working on the garage apartment every day. We're waiting on several cabinets, and one window that had to be replaced as it had a crack in it. All in all, things will take another three weeks. Thanks for the call. I'll talk to you

later. By the way, the fountain looks fabulous!"

Adam had come to clean, put tables and chairs together, add finishing touches to displays, and help polish the hardwood floors. We unloaded items and stocked the shelves in the gift shop.

The week of the grand opening was busy. The tea room would officially open on August 9, my mother's birthday. Ann and Frank were coming in for a few days to help stack supplies on the shelves and work with the wait staff.

I opened for a few hours on August 7 for our "Complimentary Come in and Taste". We had twenty people come in and order, plus Hilliard and several worker friends showed up to sample a cuppa tea and scones. Events were planned for the first week.

Mrs. Arbuckle from the BIL (Bureau Improvement League) was one who came to sample the tea on our practice day. She walked up to me, not shy at all.

"You must be Victoria Thorn, oh, that's right, it is now Storm. I knew your family well." She looked around the tea room and I could almost see the wheels turning in her head. "I like what you've done with this old house. I'll be here often. I love the sign you have over the door."

"Mrs. Arbuckle, it's wonderful to finally meet you. I have spoken with you on the phone so many times to make arrangements. The sign is something I felt would reflect the feeling of the tea room. I read the book *Three Cups of Tea* by Greg Mortenson and David Oliver Relin and was impressed."

"What it says is meaningful," commented Mrs. Arbuckle as she recited the sign: "The first time you share tea, you are a stranger. The second time you take tea, you are an honored guest. The third time you share a cup of tea, you become family." I'm going to be family."

I couldn't resist giving her a warm hug.

Things went smoothly for the most part. I visited each table and shared the making of teas, offering scones and little sandwiches.

The night before the grand opening, I couldn't sleep. I had made myself a cup of Citrus Lavender Sage Herbal Tea. A blend of fruit—floral of orange, sweet pineapple, red delicious apples—complemented and softened to a smooth perfection with lavender, sage, and sea buckthorn. It should have made me relax. Damn. It wasn't working.

My house phone rang. I must have jumped a foot. "Hello."

"Don't forget to put Mr. Ted Bear on one of the seats in the tea room." The phone disconnected immediately and I was left looking at the receiver. "Who is this?' I asked. This was on the house phone, not my cell. "But, thanks for the reminder." I went upstairs, grabbed Mr. Ted Bear, and sat him in one of the chairs around a small table in the back. I wondered if grandmother had a Mr. Ted Bear in her tea room, sitting up so proud, surveying the room, watching for those who didn't raise their pinky as they drank from a cup. How silly that sounded and how excited about tomorrow I was. Ann and Frank would help with whatever was needed. Opening days could be hectic, but I was ready. I said out loud, "Wishing we have a very busy and successful opening day."

When I finished my tea, I went upstairs and tried to sleep. It didn't happen. Not tonight. I sat in my favorite barrel chair and closed my eyes, said a few words of prayer, wishing, and soul searching. The room was suddenly cool, the temperature dropped. My neck felt a cold draft. My soldier appeared at the far end of the room. As before, he was not clear at first, but within a few minute his edges turned solid. "Be careful what you wish for…" he said, then disappeared.

What had I wished for? A busy grand opening, lots of local people visiting and enjoying themselves. And Mr. Bear presiding over all. Oh yes, and that my mother and grandmothers would watch over me for the next few days of my new and exciting adventure. I felt a chill down my spine. A little unnerving, to say the least.

I settled into my bed but continued to think about my soldier and the coldness of the room and his words of wisdom. I finally drifted off. In what seemed like only minutes, my alarm sounded and I jumped up with a start, showered, and dressed. I knocked on Ann and Frank's door and said I was headed downstairs to start the cooking and get things ready. It was here, the day I'd been working towards for so long. It seemed almost unreal, but oh, so exciting.

Sam was already baking cranberry scones and had brewed a pot of tea for us. I'd made the soup the day before but needed to add fresh chicken and warm it up.

I placed the 'open for business' sign on the front lawn. I had done all I could think of to promote the grand opening. When I opened the front door, there was a shiny penny, heads up. *Thanks mom. Happy birthday, it is your day!*

At 10:00 we opened the doors. One of the first to enter was Mrs. Arbuckle and her friend, Miss Lamb. It turns out they both were old Metuchenites. Betty Lou James from the real estate office followed them in, with Nellie from the thrift store. It was going to be like old home week. I took a deep breath and we were off and running on the first day of the opening or maybe I should say the re-opening of the Bonnie Neuk.

"Mom, what tea are we going to brew? asked Ann.

"Let's do some black Nilgiri from India medium

strength and Formosa oolong from China. Also some Earl Grey. I have my white bean and lime chicken soup, and cucumber and watercress sandwiches. Sam's cranberry scones came out hot from the oven and added a sweet touch to the meal. Devonshire cream will complete the presentation." I said enthusiastically.

The fountain and porch area looked wonderful. We had several lights placed near the water of the fountain which added to the ambiance. I had found a beautiful angel statue now situated next to the fountain among the shrubs. We had people enjoying the view of the pond area and the orchids, as well as the food.

As I ran to the back storeroom for more tea, my phone rang. I hesitated to answer it.

"Did you have Mr. Ted Bear presiding over the tea room?" and the phone went dead again with no data showing.

I yelled into the phone, "Yes, Mr. Bear is checking things out." I immediately put the phone down and mumbled under my breath. I needed to either have my new iPhone checked or maybe just throw it away!

As the customers left, many said how much they enjoyed the food and tea. Someone asked about the "bear" at the far table. "His name is Mr. Ted Bear and he's a special friend of the Bonnie Neuk Tea Room."

All in all, it was a successful grand opening. We had more than a hundred customers. I was exhausted.

We all settled in for a good night's sleep, but my mind kept going. I replayed all the events of the day in my head. I was about to nod off, when I noticed the smell of lavender and felt a draft. I immediately sat up. Across the room Derrick appeared. His image hardened and he asked, "Did your wish come true?"

"Yes, we were busy with lots of customers, hopefully returning ones. Thank you for your encouragement." He nodded and was gone. The room returned to its normal

temperature. I smiled, closed my eyes, and fell into a peaceful sleep.

CHAPTER 20

Cuppa is an informal British term for
'a cup of tea'.

The first week was hectic, but successful. Walking over to a table near the window, I greeted Mrs. Arbuckle. "It's nice to see you again." Mrs. Arbuckle was eighty years young and enjoyed being the center of attention. She had scheduled a tea for some of the BIL board members and several friends. One special friend, Mrs. France, was celebrating her 100th birthday and the ladies wanted to treat her to a special luncheon. Mrs. Arbuckle had visited the tea room on the grand opening and has been back every day with different friends. A real socialite.

"Hello, Victoria," said Mrs. Arbuckle. "Meet some more friends of mine. This is Mrs. Trundle, Miss Lamb, and Mrs. Frances, our special guest of honor. I told them about your tea room and they wanted to sample your teas

and sweets. Although I'm not much of a tea drinker as you know, they would like to try some of your specialties. I don't like all that caffeine. I usually drink decaf coffee. But I love your luncheon menu, your soups, and the atmosphere.

"Mrs. Arbuckle, I'm glad you enjoy The Bonnie Neuk. We love having you here. Now I have to turn you on to teas. Do you like oranges or lemons or limes? How about plums?"

"I don't like oranges or lemons, but I do like purple plums," stated Mrs. Arbuckle with a sparkle in her eye.

"How about cinnamon, do you enjoy that flavor?"

"Oh, yes, very much."

"Well, I'm going to concoct one of my favorite decaf teas for you. I use it when I want to slow down and relax after a busy day at work. It helps me chill out. It's decaf to boot. Would you ladies like to try some?" In unison, they all said 'yes'. "I'll be back in a few minutes."

I went into the kitchen to brew several pots of my special blend of cinnamon plum tea.* It has the rich taste of currants, hibiscus, and hints of plum, with a note of cinnamon and licorice root. It tastes good either hot or iced, but I'm serving it hot to Mrs. Arbuckle.

While the tea was brewing, I put together some scones and shortbread cookies on a small plate, as well as a chocolate cupcake with a candle on it for Mrs. Frances. With the teapot in one hand and the sweets in the other, I went to present Mrs. Arbuckle with a new taste of tea, and Mrs. Frances with her cupcake. She didn't look 100. We all sang Happy Birthday as she blew out the candle.

"This is so much fun!" exclaimed Mrs. Frances. "I'm glad you didn't put a hundred candles on the cake. I notice there is a teddy bear in the room, just like the one in the tea room many years ago."

(* Note: I was lucky to discover this wonderful tea at The Spice and Tea Exchange in Tarpon Springs, Florida. They feature a marvelous selection of teas and will make any blend you'd like. Visit them at: www.spiceandtea.com.)

"Mrs. Frances, did you know about my grandmother's tea room, the Bonnie Neuk?" I asked with anticipation.

"I remember a few things, in particular, the teddy bear that always sat in one of the chairs. It was there to ensure we always displayed Emily Post's good manners and etiquette. I recall giving your grandmother some old dishes and cups. I had many that didn't match, but she didn't mind. In fact, she said she liked the mismatching. At my age, you don't remember everything. Let me think for a few minutes and see what I can remember for you," replied Mrs. Frances.

This is wonderful! I had confirmed some things about my grandmother's tea room. She did have Mr. Ted Bear in The Bonnie Neuk and must have given it to me after the tea room closed.

"Victoria, thanks for the extra sweets. Let me try the tea and I'll let you know," said Mrs. Arbuckle.

I had chores to do in the kitchen and said I would return soon. Cleaning up the kitchen counter tops and putting away some of the extras, I realized how many things I was learning about my grandmother's tea room from so many different sources.

I must have been in the kitchen ten minutes and, as I started to walk into the tea room, Mrs. Arbuckle came running over to me. "Oh Victoria, the tea is wonderful. You were right. I did like it. You do have a natural way with people and tea. I am delighted you opened the Bonnie Neuk and am glad you have moved back to Metuchen." She gave me a hug. "Mrs. Frances remembered your Grandmother did tarot card readings and séances in the late afternoon on some weeks with some of her old cronies. Wouldn't that be fun to do?"

"Mrs. Arbuckle, I was considering something like that. I'll be having tea leaf readings, too. I've taken a class and will be starting soon."

"Oh. How exciting! Please let me know when you start

and I'll be here with bells on. I'd love to have my leaves read. Just for fun, mind you," stated Mrs. Arbuckle with a broad grin and a wink of her eye. She was devilish even at her age. I would have to start readings soon. Well, why not right now?

"Tell you what, Mrs. Arbuckle, let me go in the kitchen and I'll brew some more of that yummy Cinnamon Plum, but this time we'll leave the leaves in the pot and I'll read your leaves. Please understand I am rather new at it."

I brewed more tea and returned with the pot and my cheat sheet for reading leaves. I still needed some note-support.

What fun they had as they thought about the readings I gave them. I now was confident that reading would be a great addition to the Bonnie Neuk.

"Oh, what fun, I'm going to have a visitor in the next week. I wonder if it is male or female?" inquired Miss Lamb with excitement in her voice.

"And I'm going to be finding or coming into a little money," stated Mrs. Trundle.

"This seems like many things that your grandmother did. Tea leaves reading, tarot cards, séances. I think she even read palms. Are you going to do those also?" asked Mrs. Frances.

"Tea leaf readings will be every Tuesday afternoon from two o'clock to three. A sign will be put up in the tea room to that effect. I don't think I'll do the tarot cards myself, although I'll take a course in that, but I'll contact Anne, a local tarot card reader, to see if she would be interested in doing readings every other Thursday. If I could establish a definite schedule, people could come in for tea and a reading. We'll do a séance maybe once a month. I have to contact someone and see what we can arranage. "

"Victoria, this will be a big hit, at least for many of us. I'll consider having a Tea Leaf Reading Party and maybe the BIL would enjoy something similar. Life is too short not to have fun." said Mrs. Arbuckle as she clapped her hands in excitement. "I think this will be a great addition to the Bonnie Neuk."

CHAPTER 21

"The Journey of a Thousand Cups Begins with a Single Sip."
Art of Tea

Tammy had been in the Bonnie Neuk several times since the grand opening. I'm not sure whether she liked the tea or the buzz in the room. It had been busy from opening to closing each day. A good thing, mind you. I'd done my reading during the first week on a Tuesday afternoon. It went well. Many people wanted their leaves read and laughed and had fun. The tarot cards were scheduled for Thursday afternoons starting in two weeks.

Tammy pulled me aside. "Victoria, you'd mentioned you might consider having a séance. I found a person who had gone to a séance and said she thought the medium was genuine and authentic in her spiritual connections. I have her card and maybe we can try it out with a small intimate group," she said handing me a card with the name and number of Mrs. Betty Grafton.

"I see she lives in Plainfield, not far away. What would you think of having it after hours at the Bonnie Neuk, say around 8:00ish? They're always better done when it's dark. Atmosphere, you know. I'll call and see how many people can attend and when she would be available. I'm thinking you would be interested?" I said with a giggle and a wicked smile.

"Why, of course, I'd be the first one there. I'd love to see if I can connect with my mother or grandmother," said Tammy. "That sounds cool. You could serve tea martinis, like there is such a thing."

"There's no drinking during the séance. But don't laugh. They do have tea bags to make martinis and other drinks. I ordered some for the gift shop to see if people would go for them. And, ha ha, for me to try," I said sheepishly. "I do like my tea and I do love my martinis. Why not together? Maybe I'll use all of you as guinea pigs. Tammy, you're the first one on my list of people to include. I know you're going to enjoy the fanfare and ambiance of the séance."

"I'll ask Stacy and Sam. I'm not sure if Liz would enjoy it, but I guess I'll include her. She is such a non-believer in ghosts and spirits. I have a few customers who said they might be interested, Mrs. Arbuckle and her friend, Miss Lamb. They could be my grandmothers, but they are full of piss and vinegar. That makes seven. I'll call and see how many she needs and when she can schedule us."

I finished putting things away, sat down, and called. "Hello Mrs. Grafton, Victoria Storm from the Bonnie Neuk Tea Room. I'm interested in holding a séance."

"Hello, Victoria. Nice to speak with you. It's best to use a round table with six to eight people. You'll need candles, low lighting, cinnamon or frankinsense incense, and people with open minds. I charge two hundred dollars for a one hour session plus extra time and have an opening next Thursday. We'll see how receptive the spirits are for you and your friends."

"That would be great. Is there anything else you need me to do to prepare?"

"You'll need to clear your minds and be open to the spirits. We'll hold hands and breathe deeply to release all stress. I'll explain more of the procedures of the séance when I get there. That way, everyone will be on the same page." In the next breath she commented, "I've heard about your tea room, Ms. Storm, and can't wait to experience it." She bid goodbye and said she would see me on Thursday.

I jotted down the people I wanted to invite and called them to extend a personal invitation. I needed to confirm each person's attendance.

"Liz, hi. I'm having a séance party on Thursday evening in the tea room. I'd love you to come, but know you have your issues with spirits. What do you say?"

"Thanks for asking, but you know I don't believe in ghosts or communicating with the dead. I'm not a believer of such things, but for amusement purposes, as they say in the fine print, I'll come."

"You never know, maybe you'll communicate with your parents or someone else in your family. All you'll need is to open your mind to the possibility and allow the spirits to come in. Can you do that?"

"I think I can keep an open mind, but let me ask you something. Why does anyone want to contact the dead or have the dead contact them?"

"Some of the reasons are to give closure to a family member; to make sure they're happy and not in pain. The spirit can protect the living by watching over them, or help them in their everyday life."

"That sounds like a sensible definition. Why do you need someone, a medium, to orchestrate the connection?"

119

"The average person has no concept on how to connect to spirits. A medium has the sixth sense to communicate and repeats what is being said. She may even have one spirit she always communicates through. She relays what is said to her guests and knows how to protect the circle from evil spirits."

"I guess I'll come. If nothing else, I could watch you all and have a good laugh. I'll try and keep an open mind. I don't believe I'm doing this," Liz expounded in her matter-of-fact manner.

"Liz, you need to be open with no negative feelings or thoughts. I'm sure you can do that."

I called everyone else. Sam could not make it, but the others said they would be there. That made a total of six people. A good number to be seated around the table with open minds to accept the spirits.

I'd been busy meeting new clients the week after the grand opening. There was a steady stream of people. Some new and curious and many repeat customers. I was looking forward to evening when I could put my feet up for a few minutes. I had forgotten that my son, Anthony was coming to help on that weekend until he was at the back door with a smile and a bouquet of flowers. What a love! He helped me finish cleaning up and putting the tables and chairs in their places. I heated some white bean and lime chicken soup and served a few sandwiches left over from lunch. I also warmed up some raspberry nut scones that Sam had baked with Devonshire cream. Anthony polished those off in an instant.

He was a big help. "Let's open some of these heavy boxes and move the large armoire. It will be better over on this wall," he said. "Maybe we can also re-arrange some of the shelves and cubicles for the displays of tins and cups so they will appear less crowded."

It is always comforting for me to spend time with my children. Each one is unique. The weekend was gone before I knew it, and the next week flew by with each day more hectic than the last. Not that I'm complaining, mind you. It was rewarding to see us busy in such a short time. Hilliard called and left a message he'd like to do dinner soon, but I called him back and left a message that it would have to wait until next week. Crazy busy.

Before I knew it, it was Thursday and time for our séance. There were things to do to prepare. Mrs. Grafton had discussed the items needed to be in the room. She had said that everyone attending needed to wear loose clothing. She advised no extra jewelry, no watches, no cell phones. Purses and bags were to be left outside the table area. No heavy perfume as spirits sometimes bring a scent with them. I remember that when Derrick appeared, the scent of lavender was present. Water is important, so I filled a large glass bowl on the table. This would absorb contaminates from the air. I put three candles on the table as the séance is held in darkness.

It was almost eight o'clock and everyone seemed to arrive at the same time. Mrs. Arbuckle and Miss Lamb came together. Mrs. Arbuckle was laughing and scrunching her nose up which she does when she is excited.

After everyone arrived, we sat in a circle around the table. The candles on the table gave an eerie glow to the room. I had some soft background music playing. The medium instructed us to hold hands but not touch knees, and gently take several deep soul-searching breaths, let them out, clear our minds of stress, and think of love and peace. The medium explained she had her own spirit guides she would communicate with and who, in turn, received information from others. I found it some-what difficult to empty my mind and think of nothing. I smelled a hint of lavender, could it be Derrick?

"Take a few deep, cleansing breaths and relax. Our goal for the evening will be to communicate with family members and friends." Mrs. Grafton said a clearing prayer. "I would like everyone to visualize the circle encompassed by protective, white light. My spirit guides and I will guide the séance and will be fueled by the combined energy of the group." Because I was the person most anxious to contact someone, I was seated at her right hand for maximum energy.

"Victoria, I have a sense that you have capabilities in communicating with spirits. Is that true?"

"I'm not sure if I can communicate with many, but I have a ghost who lives in the Bonnie Neuk and follows me and talks to me." Everyone glanced at me in surprise.

"You can communicate; you have the ability. You should use this ability and see where it leads you. I feel there is something important to be discovered. Keep the communication open."

A coolness came over the room and the temperature dropped at least ten degrees. Mrs. Grafton seemed to be in a trance.

"My spirits are saying they have someone here who wants to speak with Elizabeth." Liz, the skeptic, let out a noise as she took in a deep breath.

"Auntie Libby wants to know if you have ever found the cameo necklace your mother lost"

"Oh, my God. How did you know my mother lost the family cameo? This is unbelievable," Liz replied with tears in her eyes. "My mother has anguished for years about that cameo." She was noticeably upset and kept trying to release her hands, but I kept holding tight so that we wouldn't break the chain.

"Auntie Libby suggests you move the dryer out and

check underneath it," stated Mrs. Grafton in a matter of fact tone.

"I'll try that when I go to my mom's house. Thank you," I could see she was definitely confused. I know she didn't believe the cameo was under the dryer, nor did she believe that Auntie Libby was talking, but how did Mrs. Grafton know there was a missing cameo or who Auntie Libby was?

I think Mrs. Grafton sensed there was a question in the air. "The spirit was able to connect with your Aunt Libby and transmit the information." A hush came over the room. "There is an Aunt Connie also saying hi to Elizabeth. She asks if you are still painting and drawing?"

"I am still drawing some, but haven't painted in awhile. How did you know that I did drawings?" Liz asked Mrs. Grafton.

"Again, I am just repeating what spirit says. Spirit is saying that Aunt Connie is saying you were very good and should continue your art work. You might want to consider using your talents again."

We were again deep breathing and relaxing, trying to connect. "I am receiving a message from someone's mother, Latty Smith. She wants to thank you for the flowers you place on her stone monument each year on her birthday."

Mrs. Arbuckle let out a loud yell, "How did you know that?" With her next breath she said. "You're welcome, mom. I love you."

"Spirit says your father says hello and watches over you. " Mrs. Grafton repeated from spirit.

Again, Mrs. Grafton started breathing deeply. We all sat on the edges of our chairs. Finally, she said, "My spirit says that is all coming through at present and he says good night." She said a closing prayer, thanked the spirit, and closed the door to the spirit realm. We all released hands and took several clearing breaths. We extinguished the candles, told the spirits to go in peace, and I turned the on lights. Mrs. Grafton asked for questions or comments. Everyone was spellbound. We sat and contemplated what had happened. Mrs. Arbuckle was the first to speak. It took a moment for her to clear her throat as she was noticeably choked up with emotions of joy.

"Mrs. Grafton, tell me again how you knew I put flowers on my mother's stone?"

"I don't know these things. The spirit connected with your mother and communicated her thoughts to me, just as your father did. Then I told you what was said."

"Thank you for that. It means a great deal to me to have my mother come through and my father also."

After the séance, I asked everyone if they would like a tea-infused martini. I offered samples of Silkroad Chai, Lavender Citrus, and Lemongrass mint tea infusers purchased through one of my new distributors.

"What's a tea infuser?" asked Liz.

"A small basket that holds tea leaves. Let it sit in the vodka or what ever liquor you want for a few minutes and use your imagination to add ice and other ingredients. It makes any hour a happy hour. " Everyone, even Mrs. Grafton was interested in trying one. I put together a few different kinds.

"This is delicious. It would be a good seller in your gift store. Tea Martini, what a great idea!" said Liz.

Drinking our martinis, we chatted with excitement for those who had connected. I was somewhat disappointed that I hadn't connected with a family member, but Mrs. Grafton agreed to return for another session in six weeks. Bidding everyone good night, I told Liz I'd check in with her the next day. Well, Derrick never did show up.

I was staying on the third floor in the house because my garage apartment wasn't complete. I went downstairs and made myself a relaxing cup of decaffeinated turmeric ginger. It has an earthy aroma of turmeric, with ginger, cinnamon and pure honey. They say that people who suffer from pain and inflammation due to arthritis experience relief from drinking this tea. It's good for improving one's mood and relaxation, too. I kicked off my shoes and sat in my favorite chair to reflect on the evening. My phone rang. I walked over to where it was being charged and checked the display. It was Liz.

"I had to call you." She sounded out of breath. "Sorry it's so late. I went immediately to my mother's and looked under the dryer. I felt around, but there was nothing. Then, I started to think about exactly what Mrs. Grafton had said. She said 'move the dryer.' So I did. There in the far back corner was the cameo necklace. I can't believe it. My mother was so excited, I thought she was going to faint. Thank you so much, Victoria, it means a lot to us. But I am a little confused."

"Liz, you came with an open mind and Mrs. Grafton was able to communicate and receive information for you. I'm glad it worked out."

"Next week sometime, can you and I sit down and discuss this ghost thing? I'm not completely understanding it, but it sure was right on. Again, thank you."

I smiled as I disconnected the call, but as I placed the phone on the end table, it rang. Now what did Liz want?

"The séance in the back room was a great success. I'm glad."

"Hello, who's this?" as always, the line went dead. I sat there staring at the phone. These calls are starting to really freak me out. How do they know that we had a séance in the back room? Or how do they know it was a great success? Why am I getting these weird calls and who is doing this? Am I crazy?

CHAPTER 22

"The grandfather plants and raises the tea bushes, the father harvests the tea and the son drinks it."
Chinese Proverb

I woke up early the next morning and went downstairs to make tea. I had just ordered this new tea and was excited to try it out...the Lady in Lavender. An Indian white tea with lavender, 100% organic. No added flavoring, just tea and lavender. It smelled and tasted divine. Sipping the tea, I reflected on the séance from the previous night. It was Friday, the end of a busy week.

A breeze stirred, and it was as if I felt a touch. A gentle, kindly, soft touch... I breathed in and out and looked around. I didn't see anyone. Then his image began to develop.

"It's Derrick again. I need your help."

I walked to the other side of the room. He followed.

He tapped me on the shoulder. "Go away," I said with determination.

"Most people can't see or hear me, you can."

"Well, I don't want to. I don't want to talk to a ghost."

"You have a gift talking to the dead. You can help me."

"So my talking to you is a gift. That's scary."

"I asked you to look into my two friends. Have you had any luck?"

"I haven't had a lot of time in the past few weeks, what with the opening of the tea room and all the things to be done. I feel bad. But I'll do some Internet searching and work on a few new ideas for the tea room in the morning. Right now I have a crowd for lunch and am needed in the kitchen. I'll talk to you later." I dashed into to the kitchen, hoping no one heard me talking to thin air. It has never occurred to me that my ability to see ghosts might develop in time. I wasn't sure how I felt about it, but there was not time for self-therapy with a busy tea room. I'd have to remember to be freaked out later in the day.

"Hi Sam, what are you doing for the special scones today?"

"I thought a Chai Spice scone would be tasty. I also made chocolate chip ones, but I'll freeze some for another time."

"It sounds wonderful and smells even better. You're a great cook, Sam."

"Thanks, that means a lot. I enjoy baking. I've learned a lot at Middlesex College the last few months, but I hate where I live, too noisy. Lots of kids and parties going on late at night while I'm trying to study. Not good for me."

"Sam, I have a great idea. I'm going to be moving out of the third floor studio apartment in the next few weeks, as soon as the garage apartment is completed. Maybe you'd like to rent the studio."

"Wow, that would be awesome. I'd sure be close to work," she said and then laughed.

"I'll make up a lease. Would six hundred dollars work?"

"I'm paying more than that now. It would be great! I could be ready to move in a few hours."

"I'd think it will be two or three weeks, but I'll check with the contractors. It works well for both of us." I needed to pick Sam's brain.

"Sam, I read in a magazine that a third of people ages 18 to 34 believe in ghosts. Then from age 50 on, the percentage drops to 18 percent. Are you a believer?"

Sam smiled at me and said, "Yes!" I smiled, too. I was also a believer.

I turned around, felt a cold breeze, looked up and saw Derrick floating near the ceiling. Yes, I sure was a believer. With a fearful look around to see if Sam or anyone else was in hearing distance, I finally said quietly under my breath, "Not now, Derrick. We have customers and they might be upset if they see you floating. I said I would check tomorrow."

"What did you say?" asked Sam.

"Nothing," I said, trying to hide my embarrassment.

"No one can see me but you," said Derrick. "I'll come back later. I need to talk with you about the research project and my friends. I'm not going anywhere. Let me know." He faded away.

"I'll work on it this weekend," I said, and rushed out of the kitchen and into the tea room while looking around to see if anyone heard me. They hadn't. Thank heavens!

The tea room was busy all day and I was on my feet making sure the customers were taken care of and happy. My cell rang, but I had my feet on a chair with my shoes off so I let it go to voice mail. Several hours later I remembered there was a call I needed to check—two calls when I checked. I played the first voice mail. "Hi, Victoria, it's Hilliard. How about I pick you up at 7:00 for dinner? There's a small Italian restaurant in New Brunswick I'd like to try."

I returned the call and left a message on his phone that I'd love to see him at 7:00, but no dancing tonight. My feet were dead tired. The second call was "no data" Damn, I hadn't had one of those in some time.

Rushing up the stairs to change, I tripped on the top step and fell. A voice said, "Are you all right?"

I looked around and saw Derrick floating on the ceiling. "I'm fine, thanks," I murmured.

Hilliard arrived and rang the bell in the back. "I'll be down in a minute," I yelled from the upstairs window. I met him at the back kitchen door. He looked handsome in his shirt, tie and sport jacket. I was wearing my long layered skirt of soft, sage material with a light weight off-the-shoulders top. I looked pretty hot, if I do say so myself. Getting into the car I commented, "Hilliard, I've had many wonderful compliments on the work you did on the fountain and garden area."

"Thanks. It did turn out rather well and complements the ambiance of the porch, canopy, and tables. You've probably noticed, we've been working in the area around the garage. We've been able to plant some of the landscaping. Everything should be completed in the next two weeks, right around the time you'll be moving in."

"That sounds great. I can't wait to see the total effect of the gardens. I'm sure it'll be overwhelming. The parking lines have been marked, and I've been able to use eight to ten parking spots from the next-door office building. I've agreed to repave and clean off the snow when it comes."

"Sounds like a good deal for you and for them."

We chatted the rest of the way to the restaurant and continued during dinner. We ate, talked and relaxed.

Back at the tea room we did the "huggy face-kissy bear" thing for a long time. I did fit into his arms quite well. It was comforting to be in someone's arms again. I'd missed that. We finally said goodnight and I went upstairs. I'd be glad to get into my own place. Hmm. Real glad.

I was tired, but my mind wouldn't shut down. Tomorrow I would begin the research for Derrick and do some mental planning. Finally, my thoughts drifted off to a peaceful sleep.

CHAPTER 23

"When stirring your tea, never touch the cup with your spoon. Instead, swirl the tea in the center of the cup."
Anonymous

Bright and early Saturday morning, I started on the project for Derrick. I was trying to locate his friends and do some research on the history of Thomas Edison, his lab, and an apparatus that would allow communication with the dead. There must be a connection.

I discovered that around 1925, Edison told a reporter he and his lab assistants were working on a ghost machine that could connect with spirits of the dead. He called it a spirit phone that would let the living communicate with the dead. Many major newspapers and magazines in the country leapt to cover this invention. The magazine that covered the story received over six hundred letters about using the machine. However, a year later Edison admitted he had made the whole thing up. The research stated

they never found any evidence of a schematic or machine prototype. Many felt that Edison was just playing a joke on the reporter. The article stated that the lack of a prototype or blueprints did not necessarily mean it was a hoax. But most came to the conclusion that it didn't exist. Interesting! Was he making up the report, or covering up the possibilities that someone else was working on it and wasn't having any luck and he wouldn't have gotten credit for the discovery? Something to consider.

I'd checked for names using the old fashioned sources—phone books and neighbors, if I could find an address. I went online and searched for missing people. Nothing special surfaced. Derrick had mentioned he and his friends had worked at the Edison lab, so I decided to give the museum a try. The lab was not there anymore, but they had opened a museum to house many of Edison's inventions and memorabilia.

"Hello, this is Victoria Storm. Do you have a historian at the museum I could speak to?"

"Yes we do, but I'm sorry, she won't be in until Monday morning. Can you call back? Or maybe there's something I can help you with?" asked the male phone operator.

"I'm interested in two former employees or their families. They worked at the laboratory around 1938. I'm looking for an address, their family, or some other way to locate them. I'm not sure where to begin."

"This is as good a place as any to start. What are their names? I've lived in the area all my life. Maybe I'll recognize them."

"Sam Compton and Arnold Stump. They would be about ninety plus years old now. Most likely they're deceased, but I'd like to find their families."

"The name Stump doesn't sound familiar, but Compton is a local name in Edison and Menlo Park, maybe even Perth Amboy. Check online for older directories. But call back on Monday and speak with the historian, Emily

Jones. I'm sure she'll be able to help you."

Going on line, I checked old phone directories and found several Comptons with local numbers. Excited, I placed the phone calls. The first number was a recording. The number was no longer in service. Damn! I tried the second and got an answering machine. That was encouraging... I left my name and number. I guess I would have to wait until Monday and call the museum again.

Early morning on Monday was time to prepare the soups and other foods for opening. We had fallen into a nice pattern and it was working well. Sam was baking buttermilk blueberry scones. They smelled delicious. Making myself a cup of tea and grabbed a blueberry scone to tide me over, I went upstairs to make some calls to check on orders I'd placed for tea-related items for the holidays. A few new items were needed in the gift shop for Thanksgiving and Christmas. But mainly I wanted to call the museum.

"Hello, is Emily Jones there?" Several minutes passed.

"Hello, this is Emily Jones, may I help you?"

"Yes. Victoria Storm, I own the Bonnie Neuk Tea Room in Metuchen, and I am trying to locate two old employees at the lab or their families. One is Sam Compton, the other Arnold Stump. I'm helping out a friend." That wasn't quite a lie, but I wasn't going to say it was for a ghost.

"I'll do a little research on the names and call you back later this afternoon or tomorrow."

I again gave her my phone number and hung up. I figured Tammy might be over for lunch. She'd taken to stopping by several times during the week to catch up on things and visit in the kitchen to watch the prep. But I think she wanted to taste some of Sam's new scones. I

no sooner thought that than in walked Tammy.

"Hi. Figured I'd stop for a few sweet treats."

"Hi, Tammy. Sam's made delicious Lavender Blackberry and Buttermilk Blueberry scones for today's special. Are you interested in trying one?" I said with a trace of a sarcastic smile.

"That sounds great. I'll try one of each. What's the soup for today?"

"Pumpkin Bisque."

"Sounds great."

We sat in the employee area to enjoy the smells. She was beginning to be my master taster for new items. I did value her opinion on foods.

"Victoria, I know we've scheduled another séance, but I was wondering if we could do it sooner, rather than later. I enjoyed that night and I think everyone else did too."

"You know, Tammy, I've been thinking of asking Mrs. Grafton if she would consider doing a séance on a monthly basis at the tea room. I'd open it up to others in the tea room who might be interested. I could charge $50 per person. That would cover my cost plus a little extra. What do you think?"

"You're thinking of advertising the séance in the tea room?" asked Tammy.

"Yes. I figure I could have eight guests. Some of the regulars and some new people each month."

"That sounds like a great idea. Put me down."

"I'll call her this afternoon and run the idea by her. I think she'll be interested. This would give both of us added income each month. I'd also have something else to interest my customers at the Bonnie Neuk."

It was late in the afternoon and I went upstairs and called the museum again and left a message for Emily, then called about the séance. Never a dull moment as my mother would say. Love you, Mom.

"Hello, Mrs. Grafton this is Victoria. Our plan was to have you return to the Bonnie Neuk for another séance. What would you say to making the séance a monthly event at the Bonnie Neuk? I'd advertise for new people and see what happens. I know some of my friends that came to the séance last time would love to return."

"That sounds interesting, Victoria, and I think it might work. We'll test it out. Let's schedule the event for next Thursday, and you can make the announcement that we'll have one event the following month. See what happens. Should be do-able."

We discussed the financial end of it and we both felt it would be profitable. "Sounds like a good business deal, Mrs. Grafton. Next week on Thursday it will be. I'll put up signs and talk to several of my steady clients. I'll call Sam, Stacy, Liz-maybe, Tammy, Mrs. Arbuckle, and Mrs. Lamb and give them a heads up. I'm excited."

I wanted to phone my neighbor's daughter about the event, she had attended one of my tea leaf readings and thought it was cool. "Hi, Mary. It's Victoria Storm from the Bonnie Neuk. We'd spoken several weeks ago in reference to the séance at the tea room. We're having another one next Thursday. I know you had shown some interest in the past."

"Thanks, Victoria. Sounds great. Next Thursday. I'll check my calendar and get back to you tomorrow. I'm sure I can," said Mary with enthusiasm.

"I met your dad a few days ago. He was out walking the dog."

"He's something else. I know he loves that old dog, but I swear he talks to it and expects the dog to answer. Or maybe he's talking to himself. I don't know."

"Yes, he does talk to that dog. I said hello to him and he grumbled it was a terrible day and it was suppose to rain. He is such a curmudgeon. But kind of funny about it."

"That's a good word to describe my dad, a curmudgeon.

That's what happens when you get old and can't hear. He's harmless though." Mary emphasized.

"Let me know, so I can put your name on the list."

She called back minutes later and said she would love to attend.

It was near closing when the phone at the desk rang. One of the waitresses picked it up. "It's for you Victoria. An Emily something from Edison Museum," she said.

"Hello, Emily Jones. Thanks for getting back to me."

"I was able to find a little information on both employees. Both men are deceased, but I have the last known address and a phone number." I wrote the names and numbers down—phone numbers for both families. "Not sure if they're still valid as they are old, but I've given you what I have."

Arnold Stump was the first call I made. His son explained that the senior Arnold Stump had died over ten years ago. He knew nothing in reference to the experiments I'd mentioned. He told me where Mr. Stump was buried and I thanked him for his help. He offered to check with other family members and took my phone number.

Next, I tried Samuel Compton. The number I had was for his grandson, Fred Compton. I left a brief message, but I wasn't holding out much hope. I'd talk to Derrick tonight. I'm really going to talk to a ghost about this!

The day had been busy and I was exhausted. Time for a hot cup of Lemongrass herbal tea. It has the delicate Meyer lemon citrusy taste with a slight hint of sweet ginger and a floral fragrance. It was rewarding to put my feet up, close my eyes, and smell the aroma.

"Derrick, are you here?" I asked, laughing to myself that now I was calling out to talk to a ghost. The room turned cool and a hint of lavender was in the air.

"I am here."

"I did some searching and found a little. Many had felt that the article about the spirit phone was a hoax. But I was able to connect with Edison Museum and got some information for you."

"I knew you were good at finding out things."

"Both friends are dead. Maybe you can get the Google Ghost phone directory and try calling them."

"Be real!"

"Sorry, only kidding. I spoke to the families and they don't know anything about the machine, but they promised to check with other family members. I'll continue working on it and keep you in the loop."

"Thanks. That tea smells really tasty." And he faded from view.

Should I have offered a ghost some tea? Am I crazy?

CHAPTER 24

A Loving recipe for a Perfect Cup of Tea
1 Willing friend who loves to sit and share
1 Grateful heart to have a friend that cares
1 Beautiful garden to show us God is near
Anonymous

Another week had gone by in a flash. Time for our second séance. This one was announced at the tea room and had several new persons attending. From across the room, I heard my phone ring. I'd let it go to voice mail and then checked it later. It was Hilliard wishing me success and fun for the night. Life had kept me so busy, we hadn't seen much of each other, but that would change shortly, I hope.

Mrs. Grafton arrived first to make sure the room was set to her liking. All eight people were present; Stacy, Tammy, Sam, Mrs. Arbuckle from the first séance, and Mrs. Cummings and Mrs. Wentworth, who were new, Mary from next door, and me. I was anticipating a good evening.

We all sat around the table while Mrs. Grafton explained what we needed to do. With new people attending, she wanted to make sure all hands were held to connect to the energy. She explained that this helped to strengthen the communication with the spirit. "There is a full moon tonight, so we are hoping for extensive connection." She uttered her clearing prayer and went into a trance.

"Spirit has someone trying to connect with her granddaughter, Grandma O'Reilly is here."

Tammy was visible excited. "I was named for my grandmother. I didn't know her. She died the year I was born."

Through Mrs. Grafton, spirit spoke, "You have grown up to be a proper and loving women, my dear. I am sorry I wasn't there on earth to be a part of it, but know that I have watched. I see you are wearing my pearls. Know that I love you, my namesake."

"Oh, Grandma O'Reilly, I love you, too." spoke Tammy in a shaky voice filled with love and excitement.

Mrs. Grafton took several deep breaths. "My spirit has someone wanting to connect with an Emily Wentworth. It is someone by the name of Mr. Barnes. He's very shy. Does this make any sense?"

Mrs. Wentworth spoke up, "Oh, yes. I knew a Mr. Barnes. I used to date him many years ago, but he moved away and we lost touch with each other. I didn't know he was in the afterlife. Hello, Howard."

"My spirit says Mr. Barnes is saying he is so sorry he left with little explanation. He has always regretted his fast exit and lack of communication with you. He is saying that his family had a tragic death and he left for Seattle as quickly as possible." Mrs. Grafton took a few deep breaths and continued. "My spirit says while in Seattle, Mr. Barnes was helping his family when he had an automobile accident, was in a coma for weeks, and then died. He says he cares for you and is sorry he could never tell you. He is with you even now. Does that make sense?"

Mrs. Wentworth was noticeably upset. Her eyes welled up with tears. "I always thought he didn't care about me. I'm so sorry, Howard. I really cared, too."

"Mrs. Wentworth," asked Mrs. Grafton, "do you have any questions?"

"No questions. I appreciate just knowing that he didn't forget about me. Thank you so much for the information. It really helps my heart to know."

Four spirits came over. I figured we would be done soon.

Mrs. Grafton took several more deep breaths and stayed in the trance. "Spirit is saying there is a woman named Martha Bates saying hello to her daughter."

"That's my mom, "said Mary with tears in her eyes.

"Spirit says she is at peace and wants to make sure you are taking care of your dad. She is saying "He is a handful and is lost without her."

"Isn't that the truth. Yes, mom, I'm sure trying to take care of him. I love you."

Mrs. Grafton blinked and stayed in the trance. 'Spirit is getting someone who is anxious to come through. I'm not understanding this. He says his name is Compton, Samuel Compton, and he is talking so fast. Something about an apparatus or a machine. Does that make any sense? Victoria, he wants to communicate with you."

I was so excited, I almost couldn't speak. "Samuel, you were friends with Derrick and Arnold at Edison Lab."

"Spirit says he was friends and cohorts with them both. He is speaking so fast, spirit is having a hard time understanding what he is saying. Please slow down."

I couldn't keep quiet and came right out and said, "Derrick has been asking about the machine or invention you were working on. He wanted to know what happened to it or where it is. Do you know anything about it?"

"Spirit says that he and Derrick were best friends and, yes, they all worked together at Edison Labs. They were working on a spirit phone or electronic voice apparatus to call the dead."

"Do you know where it is? Did you continue on it? Does it work?" I asked quickly.

"Spirit says that after Derrick's death, they worked on it for a while, but really didn't get it to function correctly. They showed the machine to Edison, but he had little to say at that time. Edison laughed, didn't think it would work-a hit and miss. Slow down, I am having trouble understanding you." said Mrs. Grafton. There was a quiet time and I was afraid we were losing communication.

"Samuel, what happened to the machine? Did you put it somewhere? Did you destroy it?" I asked, barely breathing in between my words, I wanted to get my questions answered and was so afraid the connection would be broken.

"Spirit says Edison wasn't paying attention and was making jokes about it to a magazine editor. Samuel says he is not sure where it is, but it might be at Derrick's house on Middlesex Avenue. He says it was in a hidden cabinet in the basement where they worked on it in the evenings. It's sort of like a phone to heaven. After Derrick went into the service and then died, interest in the machine was lost. Spirit says he doesn't really know where it is."

Mrs. Grafton took a few deep breaths and said, "Spirit says good night." She said a prayer to close and we all released hands.

I couldn't believe what I learned. Derrick would be excited that we had connected to Samuel and learned some new information about the machine. Still a question as to where it is located. Or if it was destroyed and won't be found.

Mrs. Grafton turned to me, "So Victoria, what's this

about the 'Derrick ghost' of yours. What does he have you searching for?"

"Derrick lives in the house I purchased for the tea room. He and his friends worked on a machine that he says could communicate with the dead. Sort of like you do, I guess. I'm not really sure. Derrick wants to know what's happened to the machine. Thanks to you and spirit, I have a better idea where it might be. I found a secret area in the attic with just a few papers in it. Now I'll have to do some searching in the basement."

Everyone was staring at me. There were so many questions being asked, "You have a ghost in the tea room? I've never seen or heard him. But I know sometimes you act funny, like you're talking to someone and not me," commented Sam.

"Aren't you afraid?" asked Mrs. Arbuckle.

"Not any more. I was at first," I said.

I really didn't want to go into too much detail about my ghost. I simply said, "Derrick has come to visit me since I moved in, and he wanted me to find his friends. I've had so much rebuilding and clearing out, I can't believe the secret place wasn't found. When I had my walk-through, the agent showed me a secret closet in the attic, but he said there was a second one. He did not know where. Somewhere there's another hidden space. My work is cut out for me."

Mrs. Grafton spoke to Mrs. Wentworth. "Do you have any questions or comments?"

"I really can't believe I had communication from Howard. I'd always wondered what happened. I was hoping to marry him at one time."

"Mrs. Wentworth, he cares about you and watches over you."

"Tammy, do you have any comments or questions?" Mrs. Grafton asked.

"No, I don't think so. I'm very pleased to have a mes-

sage from Grandma O'Reilly. I didn't know my pearls were hers," she said as she fingered her necklace with love.

"Victoria, you've been busy yourself. Do you understand all that information about a machine?

"Yes, Mrs. Grafton, I do. It makes my searching to find it even more interesting." They were all looking at me with disbelief and chuckling about my talking to a ghost.

I served hot herbal tea and some infused martini to everyone. Mrs. Grafton took me aside, "I think this idea of a monthly séance has started off rather well. We had a full house tonight, and hopefully next month will be the same. I'm very positive about this. We'll take it one month at a time. Also, I'm glad your ghost friend came through. What else are you not letting on?"

"Time will tell, Mrs. Grafton. Time will tell."

CHAPTER 25

*"There are few hours in life more agreeable
than the hour dedicated to the ceremony known
as afternoon tea."*
Henry James, "The Portrait of a Lady"

It was a fun evening, and in my case very informative. What was I going to do with this knowledge?

I was cleaning up in the kitchen when the temperature dropped and Derrick appeared near the ceiling. "You received news about the machine, I feel it."

"Derrick, your friend Samuel Compton came through to me at the séance. He stated you were all close friends and worked on the machine in your spare time. After your death they lost interest in the machine. He is not sure where it is, but suggests it could be in the basement of the tea room. Do you know of a room or closet in the basement?"

Derrick went into a deep thinking mode and concentrated deeply. "I'm not sure where they're talking about,

but we could go to the basement and check."

"We could try to locate the area, but I can't believe with all the workmen around here no one noticed this hidden area." Getting a flashlight and a crowbar from the closet, I started down the stairs with Derrick floating close behind.

The basement was large with several rooms and areas with shelves of all sizes, as well as the furnace area. The workmen had piled cabinets and 'stuff' for the garage apartment everywhere. I don't think I'd been down here more than once since I had the home inspections. What a mess.

"We can do a quick check of the place tonight, but I think I'll have to spend some quality time straightening this place up—and, in the process, look for the machine. The cabinets are all over the place; you can't even see the walls. These will be installed in the garage apartment within two weeks and the rest of this stuff will be going there also. Nothing is quick and easy, is it?"

Derrick and I tried to look around the walls and the floor area, even under the stairs. Nothing. The machine had waited this long for discovery, it would have to wait a few more weeks.

"We'll continue this next week." Here I go again, talking to my ghost. He nodded and floated up the stairs, leaving me to get myself out from behind the cabinets. Tomorrow was a busy day. The Red Hat Society was having a luncheon meeting.

Friday, I hit the floor running. I still had to prepare for the special meeting. Derrick came floating in and tried to get my attention. "Not now, too many things to do for luncheon."

"What did you say?" asked Sam as she put the second

tray of scones into the oven.

"I wanted to know how the scones were coming along." Did I get away with that?

"This luncheon is for the Red Hat Society, correct? What is so special about these red hats?" Sam inquired. "Do they really wear hats that are red?"

"It's an interesting story. In 1997 Sue Ellen's friend was turning 55. She wanted to give her something special. Sue had been to a rummage sale and found this bright red fedora that was really campy. She also had read a poem entitled "*Warning*" by Jenny Joseph. Go look up the poem later, but I'll recite the first two lines."

"When I am an old woman I shall wear purple
   With a red hat that doesn't go and doesn't suit me."

"The idea is for women over fifty years to enjoy humor and be silly as comic relief, making lasting friends, and helping each other. At present I think there are over 40,000 chapters. That's a lot of red hats! It stated that the official Red Hat Society Day is April 25th of each year. "

"I'm sure glad I made special scones. I put together a purple plum and a cherry version. So they'll have their purple and red," commented Sam with a big grin.

"That's super. I, too, have tried to put their colors to work. I've made a soup that has red tomatoes and purple (black) beans." There was a commotion in the other room.

"I think our guests have arrived. Sam, stick your nose out the door and take a peek at all the color that walked in." I said as I was half out the door checking them out.

One woman with a large bright red fedora and another in a small red pill box came up to me. They looked like they were in charge.

"Hello, I'm Victoria, the owner of the Bonnie Neuk Tea Room."

"Hello. I'm Janet Seld. Gosh, you look familiar. I used to go to Metuchen schools until around seventh grade then moved to Cherry Hill. I never graduated from MHS.

But glad I've moved back."

"My maiden name was Thorn. What year would you have graduated?"

"My name is still Seld. I should have graduated in 1965, but when I transferred I had to repeat seventh grade."

"That's when I graduated. We must have been in the same class for a while. Small world! We've tried to give you food to complement your color, red: tomato soup with purple beans and scones with plums and cherries."

"That's great. Thank you. I'll make sure everyone is informed of that. You really have a very unique tea room here," she said.

"You don't know the half of it," I said with a chuckle, almost to myself.

"I think I do," Janet said, then smiled a bewitching smile.

I looked at her and wondered what she meant. Maybe she felt the vibes, too.

Just then more red hats came in. There must have been thirty, all wearing some form of red hats as well as some with purple trim. What a sight to behold.

I showed them to the room and excused myself. I ran to get my camera. It would be great publicity.

Each person was getting a small cup of soup with a scone and a cup of tea of their choice.

I went in the kitchen to help Sam get things ready. Sam said, "This Red Hat Society looks really neat!"

We rushed to get the foods out before the meeting began. It wasn't until late afternoon that I had a few seconds to sit down. I needed to call the contractor to find out when I could move into the garage apartment. It would be good to have a space that was mine where I could stretch out and feel totally at home.

"Sam, I'm going to make myself a cup of Chai tea and take one of your red hat scones and go upstairs to do a little work."

"No you're not. You're going to talk to that ghost friend of yours! Does he have a Google Ghostnet? she said with a loud, belly laugh.

"He has something like that so he can check things out in the spirit world. Not sure what he really calls it."

"Damn it. I was only kidding, but he really has something?"

"I'm not going to go there, but yes, sorta."

"I think maybe during the next séance, I'll try to have Mrs. Grafton get in touch with my grandma. You know, the one whose tea set is on the shelf in the other room."

"Sounds good, Sam. We'll have one each month for a while to see how they catch on."

I went upstairs to my office, sat down, and took a few long, deep breaths. No sooner had I closed my eyes for a moment when the temperature dropped and the smell of lavender surrounded me.

"Derrick, are you here?"

"Yes, anxious to hear your findings in the basement. Did you have a chance to check with the contractor? "

"I mentioned I spoke with Samuel at the séance the other night, and maybe you can find out more about your other friend. He might have an idea where the machine might be. I didn't talk to Ron to see if they came across anything odd in the basement. They'll be moving some of the stuff out soon and we'll see.

"I'll try to rack my brain to see if I remember anything about the basement. At present I don't remember hearing anything. I'll have to do some serious thinking… I'll get back to you in a little while." And off he went and just faded away.

Victoria, you are having a wonderful discussion with this ghost! Are you crazy?

CHAPTER 26

"What better way to suggest friendliness—and it creates it—than with a cup of tea."
J. Grayson Luttrell

Ron had told me that by the end of the week I could move into the apartment. I didn't waste any time and immediately called a mover.

Sam was going to be moving to the third floor studio apartment as soon as I vacated. Probably as I was walking down, she'd be walking up. She was as excited as I was. Everything was coming together.

"Sam, I should be moving out Saturday if you want to move your things on Sunday. We can co-ordinate things."

"Sounds great. I'm really looking forward to living here. It's been getting increasingly difficult to study given the noise."

"I think it will be easier for both of us," I said. As I turned to put leftover chicken in the refrigerator, there on the floor was a penny heads up. Under my breath I said, "Thanks, Mom."

"Victoria, I've heard you say that several times. What does it mean?" asked Sam.

"It's just me thinking of the poem by Charles L. Mashburn called *'Pennies from Heaven'*. I'll see if I can find the poem in my stuff upstairs, but it might be easier to Google it. The poem is about someone who finds a penny and feels it is sent from heaven. My mother read me the poem when I was young and it has always been a connection between us. I save all my found Pennies from Heaven in a box decorated with an angel on the outside. Since my mother passed, the number of pennies I find has increased. And since I have been on the Bonnie Neuk renovation, I have found even more pennies. I just feel it is my mother saying 'hi', 'pay attention to me, daughter', 'you're doing the right thing'. Or, if it's tails, 'rethink what you are doing'. I think I feel my mom is sending me a thought, so I thank her for the thought. Silly, I know, but sometimes it is just too meaningful to overlook. Many times ghostly signs are subtle but recognizable. Often they seem like coincidence. Letting go of rational thinking and turning in to our inner mind is more difficult. Spirits can make an object appear or disappear. They are also able to move an object from one part of the room to another. It takes a lot of energy to do this, but it does happen. Sometimes they use this method to get your attention."

"I don't think it's silly. We all need to know or hope that someone is watching over us. Whether it's an angel, a loved one, or God," said Sam.

"I think you are correct on that. Very well said."

The end of the week schedule was light and nothing

had been planned for Saturday. Good for our moving, not as good for business. I had time in the evening to go over boxes and sort things out, earmarking some things for the garage apartment. The last of the cabinets had been removed from the basement so that area was thinning out. The porch addition to the garage was completed, but I won't be using the sitting area much this year as the weather will soon start to change. However, it'll look great to see the gardens, fountain area, and rear porch of the house from there. Lovely views.

CHAPTER 27

"Where there's tea, there's hope."
Sir Arthur Pinero

The move went smoothly and by Sunday night we were both settled in, but exhausted. I checked my cell phone and there was a voice message from Hilliard just wishing me a safe move and asking if I wanted to go out to dinner on Monday or Tuesday night. I'd call back tomorrow morning as I was too tired to think at present.

I woke up early the next morning and walked around my new apartment with my cup of tea. It is great to finally have a place to call 'home'. I checked the schedule for the day and there were no parties, meetings or large get-togethers planned. I called Hilliard back and left a message.

"Hi, Hilliard. Why don't you come to my new home tonight around 7:00 and I'll make dinner: a pork roast stuffed with figs, and pistachio with asparagus and risotto. Just leave a message on my cell if that is okay."

The tea room was buzzing with a steady stream of people for lunch.

"Hello, Mrs. Arbuckle. I see you have brought some more of your cronies to sample the food at the Bonnie Neuk. What are you interested in today?"

"Hello. We came to try your soup, salad and those great tasting scones. What are the specials today?"

"We have cream of asparagus soup with Mediterranean chickpea salad. Sam has made some lavender blackberry scones that are excellent."

"Sounds wonderful. I'll try the special. What do you ladies want?" They all agreed to have the same as Mrs. Arbuckle. They knew she was the master taster of many of the meals at the tea room. I said I'd make them some special decaf blueberry tea.

"The tea is blended with decaf Ceylon tea, natural blueberry flavor and raspberry and blueberry leaves. I know you only like decaf, Mrs. Arbuckle. This tea is just right for you." I went in the kitchen to start the blueberry tea steeping while I helped put together their soup, salad and scones. I hope when I reach her age, I am as energetic and fun loving. She really is amazing.

The day went by quickly and kept me busy. I checked my cell phone.

"I'll be there at 7:00" the message said from Hilliard. That put a smile on my face. I walked over to the apartment to get dinner started. Another call clicked in as I disconnected with Hilliard's message. *"Did Mr. Ted Bear help you greet all your guests today?"*

"Who is this?" as always, no data appeared on the display of the phone. Damn, I thought these calls had stopped. Looking at the phone, it just disconnected.

Hilliard was coming so I needed to get going on dinner. He was coming to 'my place'. That sounded nice. It was exciting. I put a bottle of red wine in the frig to cool. I prefer it chilled just a little. It took no time to put together the pistachio nuts and fig stuffing for the pork loin roast. I had to chop some fresh garlic. Oh, maybe I shouldn't add too much garlic? The smell as it cooked was amazing. The risotto was cooking slowly and the asparagus was cut and ready to roast. There was a knock at the door followed by a "hello". Hilliard opened the door and came in with an armful of roses.

"Here you go…a gift for a new home," he said handing me the large bouquet. What a love! I took them from him and gave him a big kiss, but had a puzzled look on my face.

"Thank you, they're beautiful, but I'm not sure where my vases are. I'll just use this water pitcher." I put water and the little package of flower freshener in the pitcher and arranged the roses. What a great shade of red.

I showed Hilliard around the apartment. As we went from the kitchen, to the den and then the bedroom, a smile came over his face. "How nice n' bright this room is."

"You devil," I said with a twinkle in my eye. We strolled back towards the kitchen. "Wine, Hilliard? He nodded and I poured each of us a large glass.

"Let's take the wine outside and sit on my new porch and enjoy the garden that someone special created for me." Hilliard smiled at the complement. "I have a sneaking suspicion that the last of the summer evenings have come and gone. There is a crispness to the air that speaks of leaves turning colors, pumpkins ripening on the vine, and chrysanthemums as the last flowers of autumn before the winter's icy finger might consider sprinkling snow. I won't be able to use this porch much longer. Let's sit there." We sat on my new deck chairs and chatted about the tea room, the appearance of the garden and my new home. An hour passed while the food cooked slowly in the oven. I had my new counter set for dinner.

"This pork is great! You said it was stuffed with figs. What else do I taste in there? The flavor blends so well."

"It has onions, but it is the pistachio nuts that hold the flavors all together." We chatted and ate and ate and chatted. I got up to clear the dishes and clean them.

"I'll help." As I washed, he dried. "This is a great size kitchen. Everything is so handy." Coming from behind, he wrapped his arms around me and held me close.

I began to pull away, but Hilliard held my arms in place. Then his big hands moved to gently rub across my back, urging my heart closer to his. I shut my eyes, inhaled the lavender scent of his aftershave, and the faint scent of wine on his breath. He put his lips to my ear and whispered, "Are we done cleaning up?"

"Yes, I think so," I replied breathless as a thrill went through me when his lips touched mine.

At first, Hilliard's kisses were light and teasing. They tasted of wine and the strawberries I had served for dessert. Soon after, the kisses deepened and lasted longer. His hands left my back and moved down my blouse to unbutton it. He unhooked my bra with just one flip, cupping my breasts in his large, callused hands. He was finding ways to make me sigh and moan using his tongue to run around my nipples and eventually suck hard to make them perk. And perk they did. I moaned again and settled into nibbling on his right ear and circle it with my tongue.

My head was spinning and my heart racing. In one move, he undid the zipper of my skirt and let it fall to the floor. I fumbled with the buttons on his shirt and, my lord, he was wearing cufflinks. Who wears cufflinks anymore? He moved me towards the bedroom and pressed me tight against the door as we entered. The full length of his body was pressed into mine for a little bump and grind.

"I've been waiting a long time for this," he said.

"So have I. Now that I have my own space, it makes it

more private." I said breathlessly.

There was clothing dropped along the way to the bed-room. He seemed to stay at that door too long. With one yank on his arm, I pulled him towards my bed. I fell on it and pulled him on top of me.

He looked at me with surprise, but continued with his tongue caressing my lips and sinking deep in my mouth. I was heating up fast. So was he. How long had it been? Too long! We intertwined and drank of each other in depth. Much too long...

CHAPTER 28

"If man has no tea in him, he is incapable of
understanding truth and beauty."
Japanese Proverb

I tried to convince Hilliard to stay. "I have a meeting first thing in the morning. Need to have a suit on and be prepared. Don't think I would if I stayed. Sorry, next time." He smiled a lovely good-bye.

I let Hilliard out and snuggled back under the covers. The smell of his lavender aftershave was in the air. Did he know lavender was my favorite scent? Wait a minute. The scent filled the room and a fuzzy figure appeared in the far corner. I thought he couldn't leave the house, but here he was floating towards the ceiling. "How did you get to the apartment?"

"I guess I can go anywhere on the property, including your new home. I wasn't sure I could, but I managed. Was there just a romantic scene?"

"What are you doing sneaking around and watching me? Don't do that." I said angrily.

"I only saw him leaving and assumed the rest. I'm not a peeping Tom," said Derrick.

"So, what do you want?"

"Now that the cabinets and stuff are out of the basement, I figured we could search for that secret space."

"Derrick, I've been pre-occupied with the move but tomorrow, after closing, maybe Tammy and I can check out the basement."

He nodded yes and faded away. I wanted to get some well deserved sleep. Pulling the covers over me, I grinned from ear to ear and drifted off. It had been too long...

The next day I called Tammy. I figured she would help me find that secret place. She was good at working with the ghost thing. Left a message to come over after closing for some 3 S's: soup, scone and searching.

She arrived around 5:00. "So, if you're going to put me to work, I need some substances first to sustain me during the searching," she said laughing.

"How about I heat up some asparagus soup with one of Sam's scones?"

"Sounds good to me. While I partake of the food, you can explain what you need me to help you with. We're searching the basement for a space? What kind?"

We sat down and ate while I told her about the secret space I thought might be in the basement. "Let's get going on our search," she said. "Do I have a miner's hat to fit the part?"

"Funny! No hat." I took a hammer, crowbar, flashlight, and a pair of work gloves and descended into the basement.

Kneeling down on our hand and knees, we tapped the

walls and areas under the stairs. There was a main room with several smaller ones in the rear and the furnace room. Together we moved some of the shelves that were against the wall, tapping and listening for a hollow sound. Nothing. Maybe Samuel was wrong. Then we moved into the back rooms and did the same thing. I had Christmas ornaments and a tree in the first room. We moved them and knocked on the wall. Still nothing.

We spent two hours with no success. I had some folding chairs on the wall under the stairs, so we took two out and sat down to re-group.

We sat there and looked at all the inside and outside walls.

Finally Tammy said perplexed, "See the basement windows here and there. These two have a window sill that is maybe six or eight inches wide. Look at the other wall and window. The sill is much wider, maybe fifteen inches more. Why?"

"Don't know. Let's take the crowbar and check it out." I moved the chair over to the window, climbed up with the crowbar and looked from the above angle. Six large screws held the piece in place. "Tammy, I'm going to try and unscrew this sill. Maybe there is an area underneath." I used the screwdriver, and eventually with some effort, was able to remove the screws. I handed them to Tammy one at a time. "I'm going to try and pry this sill out with the screwdriver." I pulled and pushed, but it barely moved. "Tammy, hand me the crowbar, I'll try that." The sill flew up when I put the crowbar under and tugged, then crashed to the floor. I had to go on my tiptoes to see inside. It looked like a floating shelf that had supports on four sides. There was something on it, covered with a cloth. It was too heavy to lift. I needed another set of hands. Tammy moved her chair next to mine and climbed up. Both of us were finally able to move the shelf up and set it on the floor. I couldn't wait to remove the cloth. We looked at each other. Before our eyes was something that had a phone looking attachment, a small clock and then a counting device with numbers. It was about one feet by maybe ten inches wide in a box with a cylinder made of tin foil. Could this be the 'spirit phone' from someone's imagination so many years ago?

"Tammy, this looks like the machine that Samuel and Derrick described. I think we've found it." We were both jumping up and down and so excited. Where was Derrick when you needed him? "I'm not sure what to do about this or who to tell."

"You're right. We don't want this to fall into the wrong hands. What should we do?' Tammy asked.

"I'll see if I can contact Derrick and have him look at it. In the meantime, we shouldn't say anything to anyone. I'll cover the machine and put it on the shelves in the garage. The sill should go back in the window with the screws attached, so it looks normal. Thank you so much for your help, Tammy." We hugged each other.

"I'm really excited. It was like a Nancy Drew mystery. Remember her? I won't say a word. Let me know what Derrick says? I'll call tomorrow." She put her finger up to her mouth, made as if to say, I'll be quiet and then headed home.

"I'll talk with you tomorrow," I said.

I carried the machine to the garage and carefully laid it on a shelf. Going upstairs, I sat on the side of the bed and called for Derrick. In no time I could smell the scent of lavender as his image started to materialize across the room.

"Derrick, I think I have found your machine. Come down with me to the shelf in the garage." He floated along, following me down. I moved a few things in front of the machine and pulled it to the front, removing the sheet so Derrick could get the full effect. He was astonished.

"Victoria, it's the machine. It's been such a long time since I last saw it, but that's it. Thank you so much. You really pulled it off. I can't believe it." He was noticeably excited.

"Now, what do we do with it, Derrick?"

"I'm not sure. They laughed at us many years ago, so they most likely will again. At least it is found. I really appreciate your effort."

"Derrick, we need to show someone at the Edison Museum this machine. Maybe I'll go talk to them tomorrow? "

"I don't think that is a good idea. They didn't care then, so why would they care now? Or if they do care, they'll try to steal it. Let's think on this."

I can't believe we're having this conversation. He doesn't want to do anything, and is only happy we found the machine. What should I do? Maybe Derrick is right. Do nothing, except knowing his ego has been satisfied in finding the machine. The exciting thing is we finally found it in the second, secret hiding place. Guess I'll sleep on it.

CHAPTER 29

"The perfect temperature for tea is two degrees hotter than just right."
Terri Guillements

The following day was busy at the Bonnie Neuk. We had a Bureau Improvement League (BIL) meeting for twenty women. I was making lemongrass soup and serving lemongrass tea. Sam was making lemongrass scones. It was a lemon day. During the late afternoon, I checked my voice mail and found several messages.

"Hi Victoria, just wanted to let you know that dinner was great, but the dessert was the best! I'll talk to you later today or tomorrow. How about we try that country western place we enjoyed a month or so ago. I liked the heel and toe dancing." That brought a smile to my face. We both needed more practice.

The other message said, *"Mr. Ted Bear wants to make sure all the women follow Emily Post manners."* Once again no data was listed on the area for the phone number. Who is this? I guess things were just piling up and making me crazy. How can I find out who this is?

I figured I'd do some research about Edison, his findings, and his inventions. Maybe that would give me some answers to so many questions. Internet, here I come.

Thinking about Derrick, I felt like my hands were tied with this machine situation. I couldn't just forget about it, but also didn't want to do anything that would upset Derrick, such as taking it to the Edison Museum. Victoria, you're talking about a ghost. Be realistic!

"Hi Tammy why don't you come over to the tea room later today, I'll make some soup and scones and we'll chat. It's been awhile. I was thinking of making a special tea, pungent with a hint of citrus like my signature tea. Does that sound inviting?"

"Sounds great. What would you consider putting together for this special tea? Or would you make it as a 'special of the week' tea? You could have different teas each week."

"That would be a great deal of work. No, I think I'd do only a signature tea." I said.

"Just call it the Bonnie Neuk signature tea and leave it like that. I've always like blueberry," Tammy asserted in a positive way.

"Selfishly, I like Rooibos tea. You can add other ingredients to produce different flavors, such as peach and even your favorite of blueberry. That would be good; Blueberry Rooibos. Rooibos literally means 'Red Bush' in Afrikaans. It grows in the mountains of South Africa. When fermented, the leaves turn red, making a rich-colored, full-bodied tea. Adding blueberries, elderberry and rosehip can result in a sweet and luscious blend of tea which is instantly refreshing. I'll continue experimenting, but I wanted to see if you thought it was a novel idea. Thanks for your input."

We sat in the kitchen, enjoying pumpkin soup with a lemon scone. I told her about Hilliard and our experience the other night. I could tell she was glad I found someone. She suggested we go to the Metuchen Inn for a 'ladies' night out' to just sit and chat. "How about Thursday? Unless you are seeing Hilliard.

"Probably not. He was over the other night, and I pretty much wore him out."

"You wicked girl."

"I certainly hope so," I said, laughing. I'm thinking Hilliard and I have a good relationship started.

"I have tickets to see James Van Praagh in Pennsylvania. My girlfriend in Doylestown, Pennsylvania, Danielle, called and said he was going to be at the Keswick Theater. I'm really looking forward to his performance." Tammy had an uncertain look on her face. "Do you know who he is?"

"I'm not sure."

"He is a medium like Mrs. Grafton."

"Does he do things like Mrs. Grafton, talk to the dead?" Tammy asked.

"He does things similarly, but on a much larger scale. There are seven hundred people in the audience rather than six or eight like Mrs. Grafton, but not many will be recognized. I hope I am."

"That sounds really exciting. You've got the tickets already."

"Yes, Danielle has them. They are almost sold out."

CHAPTER 30

"A cup of tea would restore my normality."
Douglas Adams

The tea room was busy from opening to close. I was feeling blessed. It had been a great six months. The weather was cold so we hadn't been able to use the outside porch area for several months. It would reopen in late spring. I had taken my orchids inside, putting some in the bedrooms and some in the apartment.

I always tried to walk around to each table and talk to my customers. Today was no exception. I had welcomed everyone except for two tables in the back.

Walking over to the one table, I guess I glanced at one of the women sitting at the table. She looked familiar. Perhaps I remembered her from high school. She was staring at me as well.

"Thank you for coming to partake tea and scones at

the Bonnie Neuk. Here are some of the specials," I said reading from the list for the day.

"You're someone I knew in high school, I'm sure of it?" said the woman as she sipped her tea. "Can't put a name to your face."

"I'm Victoria Thorn, now Victoria Storm. Metuchen High Class of 1965. Where you in my class?"

"I'm René Passer Smold, also Class of 65. Now I remember you. Small world. You have recently opened the tea room. It wasn't here a year ago when I visited friends."

"Yes, I have returned to Metuchen about ten months ago, and we've been open about six months."

"I really like what you've done with this old house. I remember a sister of a classmate lived here in this house as a renter years ago. I'm visiting for five days and then will return to North Carolina, which is home now." She handed me her card with the phone number and an email address. "Let's keep in touch. Maybe it's time for a class reunion someday soon. It would be nice to see old faces."

I gave her one of my cards and said yes, we should consider a reunion soon. We continued to chat about old times.

"I see the sign indicating you have séances here."

"Once a month a group gets together and we meet for a séance."

"I'm only here for a short time, do you think we could organize one before I leave, so I could experience a séance? I have always wanted to be a part of one. This is my chance."

"I could call Mrs. Grafton, our medium, and see if she has any openings for the next few days. Maybe Thursday or Friday would work. If I could get a few more people, it wouldn't be so expensive. Would that work for you?"

"That would be great." She turned to her friends and asked if they would be interested. They both said yes.

"You would be three, I'd be the fourth and I have several friends, Sam, my pastry chef and Tammy, a friend. That would make it six people—a good number for a séance. I'll call her when I finish the last table and get back to you. Can I use this number?" I said looking at the card. Not sure if they would still be in the tea room when I returned.

I had some tea to brew and another table to visit, but I wanted to call about the séance as soon as possible. My office was in one of the bedrooms on the second floor. I walked up and made the call. She was available on Thursday and could be at the tea room at 7:00 pm. Great! This was becoming a very popular event. I went back into the tea room to see if René and her friends were still there. They were.

"René, I was able to set up the séance for Thursday. Come to the tea room at 7:00. It should be fun. Mrs. Grafton is very good."

"That was fast. I'm really excited. Looking forward to this. I'll see you then." The three women finished the last of their lunch and left.

The soup for tomorrow was going to be Pumpkin Bisque. I wanted to get a head start on it, so I chopped the ingredients and put them in the frig. I'd cook the soup first thing in the morning. Also needed to contact the accounting person Liz had given me to start putting together my taxes for the year. It would be a little more involved than past years.

CHAPTER 31

"Coffee is my wake-me-up. Tea is my hug-me-up."
Sam Title

Thursday, the day of the séance, came so quickly. I needed a few minutes to put together some scones, the wine and cheese, and our famous tea martinis that everyone had grown to enjoy and expect.

Mrs. Grafton, as usual, arrived early to set things up as she liked. Arranging the table with three candles. I had started using the battery operated ones, so there was no scent or no true flame. If someone were to inadvertently knock one over, it was not a problem.

The guests were arriving and I introduced everyone to René and her friends, Tina and Betty. Mrs. Grafton explained the usual procedure not to touch knees and hold hands.

"I want to give a bit of information regarding several methods of communicating with the spirit world. It's always good to expand your knowledge. Since the early days of the Spiritual Movement, automatic writing has been one of the accepted methods of communicating with spirits of the dead. The Fox sisters originally used knocking and rapping that spelled out letters of the alphabet into a message. The leader slowly recited the alphabet until the spirit rapped, indicating the correct letter. It advanced so the spirits would mentally communicate to the medium with a pen in hand, so she could write down what was said. I don't do automatic writing or rapping. I find automatic writing takes too long, as did the rapping method," stated Mrs. Grafton. "I have a sixth sense which gives me special power to get in touch with those on the other side. I have one spirit guide that comes to me and the spirit in turn communicates with the spirits that you are seeking. We hold hands to intensify the energy in the room so the spirits can come through." She continued to explain the steps taken for those that were new to the séance.

"I'm going to try something different this time. Each person is to write two names—first and last name—on a piece of paper of someone they wish to connect to," she said handing out the paper. "Then each person will read the names to set the integrity of the séance. We will say the usual prayer to prevent evil spirits and have the white light protect us. Are there any questions?" No one had a question; we all were anxious to start.

We each wrote the names and then read them aloud to show our intent. Then Mrs. Grafton went into her trance and did her deep breathing. It took a few minutes of breathing before she spoke. "Someone is coming through by the name of Sam Passer, he wants to speak to you."

"Oh my God, dad, it's me, René. I miss you."

Through Mrs. Grafton, the spirit asked, "Where have

you put that old wooden carved box that has been in the family for many years?"

"Dad, I'm not sure where it is. There are several places, maybe the attic or the basement. I could look for it when I return to North Carolina. What's so important about the carved box?"

"It has a false bottom. You will need to pry it up. Inside are many old coins and some Spanish gold doubloons or *pieces of eight*. They may be very valuable now."

"Thanks, Dad," said René. "I'll look the day after tomorrow when I return."

"I love you and watch over you, my daughter," Mr. Passer said and then faded.

A few moments later, Mrs. Grafton asked, "Do you have any questions?"

"No more questions, but thank you for connecting me with my dad and getting that information."

Mrs. Grafton took several more deep cleansing breaths, went back in a trance, and said, "I have an older woman trying to come through—Emily Cummings."

"That's my grandmother," said Sam. "Hello, grandma. I love you and miss you."

"Dear child, I miss you too, but I'm with you always."

"Grandma, I'm working in a tea room as a pastry chef. I'm using some of your scone recipes. I sold your beautiful tea set to Victoria, the owner of the tea room. She has it on display here for all to see and enjoy."

"You are doing well as a pastry chef. Learning too, I see. Keep up the good work. Know I am with you always." Her voice faded on the last few words and then stopped.

"Goodbye, Grandma Cummings," Sam said with tears rolling down her cheek.

Mrs. Grafton took several more cleansing breaths and I was sure she had finished. "I have Samuel Compton here. He wants to speak to you, Victoria."

"I'm here, Samuel."

"I know you're not comfortable with Derrick's decision not to say anything about the machine. I feel he is correct in this decision. Edison was not happy that we had gone on our own working on the spirit phone. He always wanted to be the one in the spotlight and in charge. He was the inventor, not us. Eventually he talked to a reporter and then said it was all a joke sometime later to discredit us. If we had tried to publicize the device, he would have tried to claim it was his. It seemed better off to just let it remain a mystery. Maybe you could find another inventor to look at the device. Someone who is into paranormal communication might help. Keep it in your garage and let it remain a secret. Maybe at some point we'll get some ideas as to what to do with it. Not now though. Talk to Derrick, but I think silence is a good decision."

Mrs. Grafton asked if I had any questions. "No, I don't have any at this time."

Mrs. Grafton took several deep breaths and was about to end the session. "I'm getting a message, slow down. I'll relay your message. I'm not understanding this. It's for you, Victoria or maybe for you, René. She says to tell you when you get older you will live in a big old house with five woman and be known as the Five Ladies of Blueberry Hill. Again, I'm just repeating what was said to me by my spirit. Do either of you understand this?"

"I think I do. That's really funny. When we were in high school a bunch of girls would get together, laugh, and say when we became old and gray and lost our husbands, we would buy an old house, maybe at the Jersey shore, and grow old there together. I haven't thought about the house idea in many years. We were just crazy kids watching our mothers grow older and thinking of ways to have more fun than they did. So we invented this little game, and had fun envisioning it at slumber parties or on the beach. Like a Blue Hat Society…interesting," commented René. I was intrigued myself and trying to remember, so I didn't want to say too much at the moment.

Mrs. Grafton slowly took some breaths and came out of her trance. "Does anyone else have any questions?"

Sam piped up and asked, "Mrs. Grafton, how do you know who is coming through and to whom?"

"My spirit guide usually gives me a name of someone. Sometimes he doesn't know and we need to ask. And sometimes we just don't know who it is as with Victoria and the house on Blueberry Hill, just now. This time it didn't matter who was coming through; but the message was the important thing. But this is not the norm."

"I don't know about you, but I'd sure like to try one of those tea martinis I've heard so much about and some of your great scones, Sam," stated René. I opened the wine for some and made the tea infused martinis for others. I was busy in the corner putting things out when René came over and in a whisper said to me. "You know one of our teachers years ago overheard us talking about the Blueberry Hill house and she laughed and said it sounded like a good idea. Women uniting for fun and pleasure in their golden years. And we are getting there more each year. Do you think it was her coming through to us? I can't remember her name. She was a health teacher,"

"Maybe it was. I like the idea, we should stay in contact and stay friends and consider it in years to come. Our own Blue Hat Society. Life has strange twists, doesn't it?"

CHAPTER 32

"Each cup of tea represents an imaginary voyage"
Catherine Fougel

We had an informative time at the séance with many new visitors attending and many people came through. It lasted longer than usual and, by the time everyone had left, I needed to relax with a cup of tea. I finished cleaning up the tea room, made acupa, and took it over to my apartment. It felt good to put my feet up and just sit with no thought of anyone. Well, that wasn't quite true. I was thinking about Hilliard and our upcoming weekend and Derrick. I closed my eyes and relaxed when I smelled the scent of lavender. "Derrick, is that you?"

There was silence for sometime. Then it was broken and a voice said, "Yes. It is me. I have been thinking and will do more thinking in the next week on the subject of the machine. You have spoken with Samuel again, I feel

it. Was there anything of interest?"

"Samuel agrees with you that nothing should be done about the machine. We shouldn't advertise that we have found something."

"We will not say or do anything right now. Changing the subject, you had talked about opening a small bed and breakfast. What are your plans?" asked Derrick.

"Funny you should ask that. I've been doing a lot of thinking about the B & B. The rooms are basically finished. I just want to add some personal touches and then do some advertising, possibly at Middlesex College and Thomas Edison College and several other local private schools in the area. Parents of students might prefer to stay here rather than at a cold, impersonal hotel. And we have a great restaurant just across the street—the Metuchen Inn. Because we are on the metro train line to Newark and New York, some business people or tourists might like to pay less than a city hotel and enjoy a small town environment. There are also several magazines where I plan to place advertisements.

"You can put a little twist to your bed and breakfast and make it a haunted B & B. I could float around and make things move which, by the way, is called apports. That is when solid objects can materialize out of thin air or ghosts can make coins, flowers, keys, or in this case tea or scones to appear or maybe disappear. We can hide a dinosaur under a coat and you won't see it. I could get with the other ghosts and we could put on—a 'Breakfast with a Ghost' show."

I laughed out loud. "Derrick, why would someone want to breakfast with a ghost?"

"You never know. There are many people out there who want to communicate with the dead. You've seen how popular the monthly séances have become. Why not a little added mystery during breakfast?"

"You're serious, aren't you Derrick?"

"Yes, it would be fun for us ghosts. I'd feel like I was adding to the experience at the Bonnie Neuk."

"Who are the other ghosts that come and go in the tea room?"

"The Merriwither's—Edna and Edward. They lived here maybe ten years ago and both died in the house, but at different times, mind you. They can come and go, but I'm sure they'd like to be a part of the 'little show'," Derrick said with a wicked laugh. "There is always someone named Carl; not sure why he comes and goes, but he does. It could be fun!"

"Sure gives me something to think about. I'll run the idea by Tammy and see what her opinion is on the topic. She's up on ghosts and haunting. Hmmm, the more I think on it, the more I like the idea. I could serve haunted apples oatmeal and 'come alive' strata." I laughed. I must be nuts.

"Think on it. I'll talk to the Merriwither's and Carl and we'll see what we come up with," he said and then faded away.

Could I pull this off and entice people to stay at the B & B and have a spooky breakfast. I sat and finished my tea in deep thought. Would this work? It would definitely add some intrigue to the Bonnie Neuk. It could increase and add more to our monthly séances. Maybe it's time to see Maria Pole again.

The next morning I needed to finish the soup and work with Sam to get things ready for the day. The more I thought about the B & B, the more it interested me. I ran up to my office and checked on several orders that had not come in yet. Then I called Tammy, "Why don't you come over for a late lunch? I have several interesting ideas I want to run by you and see what your take is on them."

"Sure, I'd love to. What's the soup today?"

"It's Pumpkin Bisque. I'm making it now and I'm sure Sam has some tasty scones to add to the treat."

"See you around 2:00," said Tammy.

"Great, see you then."

Time went fast. Lots of people lunching at the tea room. I stopped at tables and chatted with guests all the while thinking what the possibilities of this new project would mean for the tea room.

Tammy came in, saw I was busy, and she went into the kitchen. She chatted with Sam and several of the waitresses while I finished up in the restaurant. Then I scuttled into the kitchen.

"Hi Tammy. Thanks for stopping by."

"It's my pleasure. I just love all your soups. Free lunch is always good."

"I need to pick your brain on a very unusual topic that Derrick, you know, my ghost friend has suggested. Come and sit while I get your soup."

"Yes, I do know who Derrick is."

"Well, he came up with a real crazy idea, but the more I think about it, the more I'm intrigued. He asked about opening the Bed and Breakfast, which I had planned to do in the fall, but putting a haunting twist to it. He suggested he and the Merriwithers, the other ghosts that haunt here, could put on a little show. Maybe carry teapots and tea cups and be invisible, or deliver my haunted apple oatmeal. I also suggested a 'come alive' strata. Tammy, I need your intake on this crazy idea."

Tammy had a shocked look on her face. It took her a minute to recover. "Yes, it sounds crazy, but I bet it would work and I think it would catch on. There are so many people who are interested in communicating with the dead. You know how popular your séance has become over the last few months. Many people have inquired and come to experience the séance. Maybe you could have a weekend for people who are interesting in connecting. Have a séance on Saturday night and a spooky breakfast on Sunday. I think it would be a novelty. It's popular in Charleston and St Augustine, why not here?"

"That was Derrick's suggestion too, about increasing the séances. But maybe have a scheduled one or two weekends a month for special ghost-interested guests. Mrs. Grafton would like this. I'll call her later and run the idea by her."

"Try it and see if it works for a few months. You could always go back to a regular B & B. What have you got to lose?"

"I'll open maybe during the summer months when things are slower. Then in the fall, schools will open and I can advertise. I am planning on doing the bed and breakfast thing anyway. Just then my phone rang. I picked it up to answer it, no data was displayed. I haven't had a call like this in some time.

"The signature tea was a great idea." The call was disconnected and no one was on the line.

"Hello, is anyone there?" Although I knew there wasn't. They had hung up. Tammy looked at me with inquisitive eyes. "What's wrong?"

"Nothing, just one of my mystery calls. This one said the signature tea would be a great success."

"It is a good idea," said Tammy. "Most of your ideas are interesting, unique and well worth the effort."

"Thanks, I'm not crazy to do some of these things?"

CHAPTER 33

"One sip of this will bathe the drooping spirits
in delight, beyond the bliss of dreams."
John Milton

I had spent a good amount of time working on a business plan for the new adventure. Would it take off? Not sure, but it was worth the effort. There were several magazines that I could advertise in for just the bed and breakfast and two that I could describe the séances and maybe a hint of a ghost visit. I also called Maria Pole, my psychic friend, to make an appointment for Thursday. Friday afternoon I was heading to Atlantic City to the Landscape Architectural Convention and to meet up with Hilliard. He was leaving on Thursday. That should be interesting and fun. It was going to be my well deserved R & R.

Soup was completed for the day and Sam was busy making fresh chocolate chip scones. Maybe Stacy would like to come over.

"Hi Stacy. How about coming for a late lunch today. Fresh chocolate chip scones and tomato basil soup are on the docket. And I know you like those scones."

"Sounds wonderful. I haven't been over in awhile. Missed talking with you. They keep piling on more work here at the old Y-M-C-A. I'll just take the time off. Maybe we can do a Ladies Martini Night in the next few weeks. I always think that is so much fun. See you in a little while." I got busy in the kitchen and time flew. I turned around and Stacy was standing there.

I fixed some soup and several small tea sandwiches down in the area for employees near the kitchen. We chatted about life, who she and I were seeing.

"I had an idea about starting the bed and breakfast slowly during the summer months. Then in the fall advertise in several magazines to see what will happen. I'm not sure it will be profitable, but I have the rooms and they are basically ready." I wasn't sure what to say after that… "I was considering putting a little twist on it. A sort of mystery ghost weekend for those who would like to experience the paranormal. My friendly ghost, Derrick, came up with this idea. What're your thoughts?'

"Wow, that is really off the wall interesting. So, what would you do? Have him float on the ceiling and say boo, or move things across the room?"

"I was considering a weekend affair—Saturday to Sunday. I would have a séance on Saturday afternoon or evening with Mrs. Grafton and a breakfast with Derrick as an invisible waiter to serve. I'm not sure about all the particulars but that would be the general idea. Nor am I sure who would come, but I could advertise and see what happens. I could always just go back to a normal style bed and breakfast."

"You would have to appeal to a specific group of people, but I think it would work. I wouldn't be over zealous with the floating and serving but, I think if handled gently, people would feel it was authentic. I'm sure you'll get a group of people who would be interested in the paranormal exposure." We ate and continued to discuss the possibilities; she had many good suggestions and ideas that I would work on. I had some wonderful new friends.

Driving back to Pennsylvania and visiting old friends was always enjoyable. I had set up a morning appointment with Marie Pole, lunch with my spiritual friend to run the B & B idea by her, and then staying over at my daughter's. The more opinions the better. My spiritual friend, Danielle, was always objective and opinionated when it came to seeing the whole picture. I highly valued her broad vision. She might even come for a weekend just to experience the scene.

I walked into Maria's home and partook of the aromas. They were wonderful—sage was the strongest, but others mingled together to intoxicate me.

"Well, Victoria, it is great to see you again. I feel there are lots of new things going on in your life. Let's sit down and see what we find."

I gave her a piece of jewelry. She said a prayer and asked for the white light to guide her and protect me from harm and then went into trance to communicate with my aura and inner fields. It took her a few minutes to tune into my aura before she spoke.

"Victoria, you have many things that are positive in your future, many paths you can choose. Each one will be a step towards enhancing your future and your field in life. Give me a minute to scan the possibilities." She took a few deep breaths and concentrated on my piece of jewelry. "There is a new venue that has shown itself to you. Follow that path and you will have success. I feel you are in question about it. Do not question it, but follow it with enthusiasm and fortitude. You will be successful as you have the positive energy to complete it. Take each step at a time, but always go forward. I see many new avenues for you and all of them are positive. Am I making sense?"

"Yes, Maria, I understand. I have several possibilities and was not sure which one to follow. You are saying either one will be successful. I should choose the one that I feel is most important or most interesting."

"Either one will be successful. Choose the one that would most likely follow your inner feeling," Maria said. "I also see there is a gentleman in your future. You have met him, but are unsure which way to go. Remember to take things slow. There is no need to hurry. Enjoy each phase and look forward to the next step." She took several deep breaths and then smiled at me. "You are in a very good spot at present. Make the most of your possibilities and things will work out well."

"Thank you, Maria. You have given me a lot to think on and many things to look forward to." I gave her a warm hug and left.

The Blue Bell Inn had just been renovated. I arrived around noon. It really looked fabulous as I walked around and viewed all the new areas. It had changed for the better with updated tables, an outside area for eating, and a new bar with a piano. Danielle was already at the table with two glasses of wine. We hugged; it had been some time since I had seen her. We emailed and phoned, but hadn't been together for many months. That's what happens when you start your own business. She also showed me the tickets for the James Van Praagh show we'd be attending in two months.

"You look really great. Kids haven't changed your looks." I said with a grin.

She had three young children…a handful.

"You look and sound happy for the first time in many months yourself. I think you have a new man in your

life," she said with a wicked smile.

"I do have a new man, but we are taking it slow and easy. We have plenty of time. How are the kids?"

"Growing more each day and sometimes too mischievous, but that's kids at times. So tell me about your new venture that you had alluded to on the phone. I'm really excited to hear all about it."

"I've decided to go ahead with the bed and breakfast part of the house, but with a new twist. My friendly ghost, Derrick, has made a suggestion to have a haunting. We have been working on the idea. Here's what I've come up with. I will start for one weekend a month—Saturday to Sunday afternoon. Saturday we'll have a séance. Mrs. Grafton, the medium who is really authentic and very talented will do the séance. Then dinner is on their own and could be put together right across the street at the Metuchen Inn. Breakfast on Sunday would be serviced by Derrick and his friends—floating tea and scones. I'm not sure how all this will all come together, but we'll work on it and iron out the bugs." I continued to talk about the plans and some other ideas. She was definitely excited, and shaking her head yes.

"Sign me up for the first event. Here is an idea. I belong to a paranormal club, which gets together once a month. We discuss books, and tours that some have taken, or just read from brochures describing different haunted places. I could mention this event to them. I am sure many if not all would love to come. There are usually ten to fifteen that attend. That would do several weekends. How many bedrooms do you have, I forget?"

"Five bedrooms. You can stay with me if you'd like, and we'd fill the other rooms with people from your group."

We drank a second glass of wine and continued our conversation about my B & B and life and her kids and my new gentleman. What fun it is to chat and catch up with friends. We hugged goodbye. She promised to talk to her group about the new venture and get back to me shortly. Then it was off to my daughter's.

I arrived in the late afternoon at Ann's, who had a glass of wine waiting for me before we began dinner. It was good to just sit back and relax, spend some time talking things over and not worrying about the next steps in life. I have a weekend in Atlantic City to look forward too. Hilliard had left early for his conference, and I was going to meet up with him on Friday late afternoon to have a wonderful dinner in one of the great restaurants in the Trump Taj Mahal and stay until Saturday afternoon. Sam was taking care of the few items at the tea room, so I really could not be concerned about things back in Metuchen. The thought of a night sleep was appealing at this point.

After a great breakfast of pancakes, I bid goodbye to Ann and started the drive to Atlantic City. It was an interesting trip through the Pine Barrens and on the back roads leading to the shore. I had to stop several times to refer to the map although I had traveled these roads many years ago as a teenager. They hadn't changed; I just didn't remember where the turns were.

I arrived at the Taj Mahal mid-afternoon. The doorman had someone take my car for valet parking as he held the door open for me. What an amazing place. It was minutes from the steel pier and Atlantic City Art Center. How do they say it, "Location, Location, Location". It certainly was.

I went to the desk to inquire about the room. The desk had instructions and an extra key to let myself into the room. Hilliard was in a seminar until around 4:30, after which he would return for dinner. I was on my own for a little while. The bell hop took my small suitcase and showed me to the room.

As he opened the door, I experienced the full impact of the surrounding glass windows. The eighty-eighth floor had a magnificent, panoramic view of the ocean and beach. The sun flooded the room with natural light as I walked around the suite touching the soft sofa and chair. I had two hours to relax and enjoy the outstanding view. There was a bottle of wine chilling on the coffee table. Why not indulge? So I opened it and poured myself a glass.

I continued walking around the large living room and bedroom suite and then went into the bathroom. My mouth fell open. There before me in the middle of the room was a heart-shaped tub. Incredible. It was big and marble and definitely heart-shaped. Well, I wasn't going to let that go to waste. I found some bubble bath on the counter and went to work filling up the tub with warm water. I had lots of time before Hilliard was to arrive and could just lie there and relax with a glass of wine. Could life be any better? I could think and enjoy the ambiance of the room. As I looked around the room, I saw a double switch on the wall. Walking over to read it, it read: Jacuzzi. Omigod, the water would swirl. Turn it on!

I stepped into the heart-shaped tub as both water and bubbles came to my chin. Glass of wine in hand and sheer comfort. Several sips later, I put the glass on the edge of the tub, closed my eyes and just relaxed, drifting off into a peace sleep.

I awoke as a few splashes of water ran down my face. Next to me in the tub was a warm body. A firm, masculine naked male body—Hilliard and his glass of wine. He just smiled at me and I smiled back.

"I see you found the surprise and are enjoying it," he said with a wicked smile on his face.

"Hm-m...Enjoying it isn't the word. More like enveloping in it. It is divine. So glad you could join me," I said turning over just a bit to be on top of him while my lips gently caressed his. Within a moment, the touch had become a full fledged, deep kiss. His tongue moved

gently around in my mouth, heating up the situation. He put the wine glass on the ledge of the tub next to mine and took me in his arms. His hardness was evident. I mounted him, as I was on top and we entered into a wonderful, continual movement of making love for the next several hours. Talk about heaven.

"That was certainly a delightful afternoon," Hilliard said kissing my neck just below my ear.

We both climbed out of the tub, luxuriously wrapped in a big, fluffy towel, poured more wine, and stood at the windows and enjoyed the most breathtaking view— the true meaning of luxury. The sun was starting to set reflecting many colors in the corners of our room. Hilliard stood next to me, kissed my ear gently, and whispered, "Do you want to go out to dinner or would you rather stay here, enjoy the view and order from the restaurant?"

"I think dinner by candlelight here in the room would be better than great." We called room service, ordered dinner and more wine and waited for our food to arrive. We ate leisurely, drank more wine and ended up in bed, only this time he took the lead. We spent the rest of the night under the sheets in each other arms doing the horizontal mambo.

Morning came too quickly. We showered and dressed in preparation to attend one of his landscaping seminars. With pencil and paper in hand, we set off for a classroom experience. I was leaving in the afternoon, but Hilliard had another seminar that evening and a third the next morning. I needed to get back to the tea room for the start of a new week.

The seminar lasted until noon. Then we ate a light lunch, he kissed me goodbye for now and I called for my car.

I drove back to Metuchen in the afternoon, savoring many lovely memories of my time with Hilliard. For a few hours, I had forgotten about the Bonnie Neuk and my ghosts. Hilliard is definitely a keeper.

CHAPTER 34

*"You can never get a cup of tea
large enough or a book long enough
to suit me."*
C.S. Lewis

I hadn't heard from Derrick in a few days. Sitting down in my favorite chair with my new signature tea, blueberry Rooibos tea, I closed my eyes and called to him. "Derrick, we need to talk, where are you?" It took several calls, but then I smelled the scent of lavender.

"I am here, Victoria. Sorry, I've been aloof, but I needed to do some major thinking."

"What have you come up with? What do you want me to do?"

"Maybe you could call Edison Museum and ask a few questions to the curator about whether Edison ever worked on a phone machine to call up the dead. Maybe I'll continue to work on the machine and see if I can get it to work. Just another point of view."

"I'll call Edison Museum this afternoon."

We didn't have a scheduled group coming, but the tea room was crowded. Around 2:30, things started to settle down. I figured this was a good time to make the call.

"Hello, may I speak to someone in charge of the museum?" I asked.

"Our assistant manager, Tom Brown is available now, or the main manager, Sarah Turnbull, who is on another call. I can put you into her voice mail."

"I'll call back."

I waited about twenty-five minutes, called back and asked for Ms. Turnbull.

"Sarah Turnbull. May I help you?"

"Hello, Ms Turnbull. My name is Victoria Storm. I want to ask a few rather strange questions. Having done some research, I discovered Thomas Edison had invented a machine many years ago, allowing him to talk with the dead. Can you tell me if you have that machine at the museum or where it might be? I would be interested in viewing it."

There was dead silence on the other end of the line. Several seconds passed. "Many years ago a reporter interviewed Mr. Edison. As it turned out, Mr. Edison was playing a joke, having told him he had been working on such a machine. He claimed only to be 'pulling his leg'. No invention ever appeared.. However, Edison developed many devices that both influenced and changed life around the world, including the phonograph, the motion picture camera, and a long-lasting, practical electric light bulb, but nothing like a phone machine to talk to the dead. He was just playing a joke on the reporter. We even have some information in the museum making reference to the incident. Edison had a strange sense of humor."

"Could any of his assistants at the lab have done something like that?"

"No, his assistants were helping with many other

machines, but nothing like that. The whole concept of 'talking to the dead' was just a spoof," Ms. Turnbull assured me. Having already done some research, what she said about the joke on the reporter was accurate to a point. Where do I go from here?

"Thanks for your help. Could there be something in his home in Fort Myers, Florida?"

"No, his main lab was here in Edison/Menlo Park. All his inventions originated in the New Jersey, New York area. Forget about this 'speaking to the dead' machine."

I hung up still with many questions on my mind. Could this be a hidden machine that was never found or ever brought to the attention of Edison? Or, because it didn't work, Edison just passed it off as a joke. Why did Derrick think the invention was real?

I looked up and Derrick was floating near the ceiling, listening to my conversation. "Derrick, according to the manager of the Edison Museum, the article about the "phone to the dead' was just Edison's sense of humor. He was playing a joke on the newspaper reporter."

"Edison saw this machine, but he didn't invent it. We did. It didn't work at the time. He couldn't take credit for it, so he just decided to call it a joke. He wanted to make sure if we did get it working that people would think it was a spoof. Let's just put the machine away again for the moment. Maybe I can eventually get it to work. Why create problems?"

"I'll respect your desire now, but perhaps in the future we'll revisit additional possibilities. And do more research," I said. I felt bad about the outcome, but it was the correct decision for the moment. "I have talked to Tammy and Mrs. Grafton about your idea about the haunted B & B. Tammy felt it could work and Mrs. Grafton agreed to do a séance on the weekend for our special guests. So I'm working on a business plan for the opening of the Bed and Breakfast at the Bonnie Neuk with invited guests and ghosts. It would be a weekend staying Saturday mid day to Sunday afternoon—a package deal once a month to start. We'll see how it goes. I'll finish up the rooms in the next few weeks and get them ready for guests. Summer is slower and when fall comes we'll see what happens. I'll need your help though."

"I did chat with Edna and Edward and their suggestions were that we could carry a tray with a cup and teapot on it and bring it out to each of the guests for breakfast. We'll do that on Sunday morning."

"It's still in the very early planning stages, but I like it. I just hope others will and attend. Thanks for the suggestions."

"You're welcome," he said and faded away.

It had been a long day and I needed some down time. I still have soup to complete for the next day and some bills to pay. I figured I would sit on the back porch with my cup of blueberry Rooibos and just relax. The air was a bit chilly, so I put on a warm, fuzzy sweater and closed my eyes. Many things to consider.

I had accomplished a great deal in less than a year. I had ended a marriage, bought a large house, remodeled it into a tea room, started a new business, met many new friends, as well as a new gentleman who I was becoming fonder of each week. I was proud of myself. The road wasn't without bumps, but all in all things had gone well. I had inherited a ghost with the house, who I now speak to on a regular basis. That part makes me laugh, but we have become friends. Friends with a ghost! Strange, how things evolve.

I wondered what the next year would bring for me and The Bonnie Neuk. I am now planning to open a small bed and breakfast. I had just five rooms, but it didn't have to be elaborate. The house was near the train station, so I could advertize in magazines for possible out of town guests. I'd like to do some furniture shopping, perhaps giving each room a theme. I had the space. Why not put it to use? Then I was considering Derrick's idea of a haunted weekend for special guests. Lots to consider and to keep me busy. I took another sip of my tea and just let it stay on my palate. It brings to mind warm, blueberry muffins. Such a rich flavor.

Just then my phone rang. No number was displayed. I knew if I was going to say something, I needed to do it before the call was disconnected.

"Hello." I said.

"The Bed and Breakfast idea sounds really great. It will be a success."

Before the word 'idea' was completed and out of the caller's mouth, I said, "Thanks, Grandma, for your help!"

"You're welcome, Victoria." The call was disconnected and no data was displayed.

About the Author

Poems

Glossary

Menus

Tea Distributors

Tea Resources

Recipes

Photo of the Original Bonnie Neuk Tea Room

Author's Notes

ABOUT THE AUTHOR

Constance L. Hope is my given name, but I am known to most as Connie or even to some as 'Crazy Connie', or CC. I'm not really crazy, but I love to laugh and have a good time.

I was born and raised in a small borough in New Jersey called Metuchen, sometimes called "the Brainy Borough." I graduated from Metuchen High School in 1965 and am in the middle of trying to organize our 50th class reunion for 2015. Wow! Time has really flown by. And what a great time it has been. Since high school, I married, raised three children who are now grown, and divorced. I now have a life partner of twenty years and reside in Fort Myers, Florida where the weather is warm and the fruit is abundant.

My father wrote five books on the genealogy of our family—the Thornalls. In the first book, I read about my grandmother, Daisy Thornall and her tea room. When she was on this planet, I never knew that she owned and operated a tea room in Metuchen until I read it in my father's book. Her tea room was called the Bonnie Neuk and I have named the tea room in my book after hers. There are a lot of similarities.

I can't remember when I didn't want to write. In retrospect, winning the "What is Patriotism" writing contest for CAR (Children of the American Revolution) in fifth grade was what made the decision. I said to my dad, "I want to write when I grow up."

During the next twenty five plus years, I balanced raising and educating three children while working. I made a decent living, but never lost the desire to write. It continued to be my hidden passion—write a story, a novel or a cookbook. Well, marriage, children and work monopolized all of my time, but wanting to write was always in the back of my mind.

When I moved to Ft Myers in 2007, I couldn't find a job as the market was in a decline.

One afternoon I was sitting, reading on our lanai, when suddenly someone tapped me on the shoulder. I quickly turned around, but no one was there. Was I dreaming? I picked up my book again and tried to resume reading. And then a voice came in loud and clear. "Write your book. Now! Get to it! It's your time." And that is what I did.

I wrote and published a cookbook, *In Addition...to the Entrée*. It's all about side dishes. My website for the cookbook is www.cookingbyconnie.com.

Now I have written my first novel. I am intending it to be a trilogy or maybe more. Let me know your thoughts on either book. They come from the heart. My email is the bonnieneuktearoom@gmail.com and the website is www.bonnieneuktearoom.com. In the back of the book I have included recipes and teas used in the Bonnie Neuk Tea Room. Since I love to cook, I thought you'd enjoy trying some of these recipes also.

POEMS

I found a Penny

Author: Copyright © 1998 C Mashburn

I found a penny today
Lying on the ground.
But it's not just a penny,
This little coin I've found.
Found pennies come from heaven,
that's what my Grandpa told me.
He said Angels toss them down.
Oh, how I loved that story.
He said when an Angel misses you,
They toss a penny down;
Sometimes just to cheer you up,
To make a smile out of your frown.
So, don't pass by that penny
When you're feeling blue.
It may be a penny from heaven
That an Angel's tossed to you.

Warning
by Jenny Joseph

When I am an old woman, I shall wear purple
With a red hat which doesn't go and doesn't suit me
And I shall spend my pension on brandy and summer
gloves
And satin sandals, and say we've no money for butter.
I shall sit down on the pavement when I'm tired.
And gobble up samples in shops and press alarm bells
And run my stick along the public railing
And make up for the sobriety of my youth.
I shall go out in my slippers in the rain.
And pick flowers in other peoples gardens
And learn to spit.
You can wear terrible shirts and grow more feet.
And eat three pounds of sausage at a go.
Or only bread and pickle for a week.
And hoard pens and pencils and beer mats and things in
boxes.
But now we must have clothes that keep us dry
And pay our rent and not swear in the street
And set a good example for the children
We must have friends to dinner and read the papers
But maybe I ought to practice a little now?
So people who know me are not too shocked and sur-
prised.
When suddenly I am old, and start to wear purple.

GLOSSARY

Apports: Completely solid objects can materialize out of thin air through a physical medium. Often ghosts will make coins, flowers, keys, or stones appear.

Electronic Voice Phenomenon (EVP): the practice of looking for hidden voices in recorded white noise. The machine that Derrick and his friends were working on.

Ghost: the soul of a dead person that can appear to the living.

Medium: a person who serves as an intermediary between the physical world and the spiritual world.

Mediumship: the practice of a certain person: known as a medium, to mediate communication between spirits of the dead and other human beings.

Reike: a Japanese technique for stress reduction, relaxation that also promotes healing. It is administered by 'laying on hands' and is based on the idea that an unseen 'life force energy' flows through us and is what causes us to be alive.

Psychometry: the art of interpreting the psychic vibration contained in an object.

Tasseography: the art of reading the tea leaves. It is preformed by interpreting symbols formed by loose tea leaves on the sides of a tea cup.

Séance: a ceremony, where people try to communicate with the spirits of dead people. It is conducted by a medium.

Signature tea: Blueberry Rooibos tea at the Bonnie Neuk.

Spirit guide: an entity that remains disincarnate to act as a guide or protector to a living person. They live as energy in the cosmic realm or as light beings. The role of your guide is to gently, but consistently guide you via intuitive nudges to stay on track with your soul's purpose.

MENU FROM THE BONNIE NEUK TEA ROOM

The Bonnie Neuk Tea Room

I have always loved teas of all kinds. Now I know why.

My Grandmother Thorn opened a tea room in 1932 in Metuchen. It was at 913 Middlesex Ave. and it was named The Bonnie Neuk. I have opened my tea room with the same name.

My grandmother was a woman keeping up with the new women's movement of her times or maybe she was even ahead of her time. Wow, she was a great entrepreneur and a role model for me.

The Bonnie Neuk Tea Room is the perfect place for your special events such as:

Tea Tasting Party
Children and Mother's Tea Party
Tarot Reading Parties
Tea Leaf Reading Party
Mystery Party
Birthday Party
Themed Party
Small Wedding
Small Reception
Baby Shower
Séance

We look forward to helping you celebrate your special occasion!

We have fancy hats, gloves, and necklaces to make your event experience more authentic.

Delicate Desserts

Special of the Day
$4.95

Black Magic Cake
with hot fudge sauce.
$4.95

Bonnie Neuk Signature
Cheesecakes
Featured cheesecake of the Day
$4.95

Scottish Shortbreads
$2.95 each

Scones
Freshly baked
Ask about our selections
$3.00 each

Beverage Choices

Endless Pot of Tea $2.95 per person
Please see tea list for selection

Iced Tea $1.95

Flavor of the day
Iced Basil Lemonade Tea
with a hint of basil to keep you coming back for
more $1.95

Fresh Coffee $1.95

French Press
Bottled Sodas $1.95

Victoria Storm's
The Bonnie Neuk Tea Room:
'Where something is always
a' brewing'

English Tea with a Flair
"Thinking out of the Cup"
Open for Dining and Tea
Monday-Friday 10:00 AM to 3:00 PM
Special Groups or Events
By Reservation Only

Contact Victoria Storm at
732-555-1212
Or email us at
TheBonnieNeukTeaRoom@gmail.com
457 Middlesex Ave.
Metuchen, New Jersey
Website: TheBonnieNeukTeaRoom.com

The Bonnie Neuk Lime Chicken Soup

Daily Soup Special

Soups served with savory scone
Cup $3.95 - Bowl $5.95

Garden Salads

The Bonnie Neuk House Salad

Mixed greens, feta cheese, tomato, red onion,
glazed pecans and dried cranberries. $5.95

Served with a bowl of soup and savory scone.
$10.95

Twice as "Bonnie" Salad

Crispy greens topped with scoops of roasted
chicken salad and egg salad with vegetables and
fruit garnish. $10.95

Cobb Salad

Fresh greens with tomato, diced egg, avocado,
crumbled bacon, grilled chicken and blue
cheese. $11.95

Served with your choice of fresh dressings:
Creamy Cilantro, Parmesan Peppercorn, Honey
Mustard, or Champagne Vinaigrette.

We serve purified water.
18% gratuity for parties of 6 or more.

Bonnie means "Good" In Scottish
TEA TIME
at The Bonnie Neuk * Tea Room

Traditional Devon Cream Tea
Two scones served with Strawberry jam and
Devonshire cream and an endless pot of tea.
$7.95 per person

Savory Tea
Cup of soup du jour, a scone with Devonshire
cream, tea sandwiches and an endless pot of
tea. $14.95

Afternoon Tea
A fresh scone served with Devonshire cream,
savory tea sandwiches and delectable mini tea
desserts with fresh fruit garnish and endless
pot of tea. $18.95

Royal Tea
Choice of soup du jour or The Bonnie Neuk
Tea House Salad and tiered tray of delicious
fresh scones served with Devonshire cream,
savory tea sandwiches and delectable mini tea
desserts with fresh fruit garnish and endless
pot of tea. $22.95

All of our loose teas are available for purchase.
Bonnie Neuk means the 'Good Corner" or "Good
Nook" in Scottish.

Specialty Sandwiches

Grilled Roast Beef Panini
Delicately sliced roast beef topped with Havarti cheese and a creamy horseradish sauce on a ciabatta roll grilled to perfection. $11.95

Daisy's Meatloaf Sandwich
A slice of moist homemade meatloaf topped with white American cheese on your choice of bread. (My Grandmother's special family recipe!) $9.95

Roasted Chicken Salad
A generous serving of chicken salad made with celery, green onion and slivered almonds on a croissant or whole grain bread. $9.95

Fresh Egg Salad
Creamy egg salad made with bacon, piled high in a flaky croissant or whole grain bread. $9.95

Peanut Butter and Peach Preserves
Creamy peanut butter topped with homemade Peach preserves served on your choice of cinnamon raisin or whole grain bread. $7.95

All sandwiches served with chips and your choice of a cup of soup, broccoli salad, or Mediterranean chick pea salad.

DISTRIBUTORS FOR TEA

1. Rishi-Tea.com I have spoken with them many times during the writing of this book. They were very helpful and had many suggestions for teas to use in the Bonnie Neuk. I found my Blueberry Rooibos Tea through them. They have amazing teas. Some examples are Yerba-mate, Chai tea and special reserves of the world's best teas. It is shipped days after the harvest. Check out their website www.rishi-tea.com to order from them.

2. Zhitea.com 1-888-944-4832 wholesale manager Jessica will email at wholesale@zhitea.com

3. Adagio.com I have used their website to do research on teas for my book. They sent me a very nice encouragement about my novel.

4. Teavana.com 1-877-832-8262 It is fun going into their shops and just trying many different teas. I used the one in Coconut Point Mall, Estero, FL. There is an entire area called the Tea Wall filled with at least a hundred types of tins of tea. You have to see it to believe it. They will mix anything you'd like right there in the store and let you taste it. I mentioned in my book that there was a store in the Menlo Park Mall , New Jersey.

5. Teaforte.com 1-800-721-1149 Their website is www.teaforte.com and for more information try info@teaforte.com. I have used their website to broaden my knowledge of teas and its origin. I have ordered a great deal of tea through their website. In fact, the tea infused martini that I served at the séance at the Bonnie Neuk Tea Room are from Tea forte. I had ordered several kinds and tried them all. The tea infusion for drinks are Lavender Citrus, Silkroad Chai, and Lemongrass Mint. I have also used their cucumber mint tea. They all are tasty and fun to prepare. It makes any hour a happy hour.

6. Stash Tea They have a great catalog for you to choose tea from. You can order online teas. Tea for each chakra or hub of energy is associated with a particular element, area of the body and inner state.

I'm sure there are other websites for tea, but these are the ones I used to research teas and help with the writing of my novel. I thank each one for your help and assistance on my road to learning about the planting, the harvest process and the drinking of tea itself.

TEA RESOURCES

American Tea Plantations

There are four (4) American Tea Plantation listed in wikipedia.org. But in my search I found several small tea plantations that were expecting to be operational in the next year or so. Please check them out online to learn about their history and perhaps order some tea.

1. Charleston Tea Plantation.
    This is the oldest tea plantation in the US. It is located on Wadmalaw Island in South Carolina. It has the perfect sandy soils, sub-tropical climate and average rainfall of 52 inches per year. It is currently used to produce both black and green teas and exists in over 320 varieties on the 127 acre grounds of the Plantation. You can check it out on line at www. charlestonteaplantation.com or call to order at 843-559-0383 ex 4206. It has been bought by Bigelow Tea.

2. Fairhope Tea Plantation, Alabama
    This plantation is located in Fairhope, Alabama and produces a small amount of tea. It is owned by Donnie Barratt. Tea is still produced at the plantation in small quantities, and sold through a nearby gift shop. You can go to www.churchmouse. com to purchase the tea.

3. Sakuma Brothers Farm, near Burlington, Washington
    They have been growing tea for over ten years. They sell white, green and Oolong. Their white tea was reviewed on Teaviews at www.teaviews.com . They are on 5 acres in the Skagut Valley in Washington State. Check them out at www. sakumabros.com. Tea is available online at their store and several local Washington state markets.

4. Big Island Tea in Hawaii
   They were established in 2001 in Hawaii and produce whole leaf green and black teas. They have created a forest infra structure for their tea. Check them out at bigislandtea.com. They produce organic, artisan teas.

There are also much smaller farms in Oregon, Mississippi and even New York State. You can check them out on the internet.

These are Tea Magazines, some websites, and tea sites and additional information on tea.

The Art of Tea Magazine has interesting facts and pictures. Check out at www.the-art-of-tea.com

Teatalkmagazine.co.uk

Margaret Thornby's Tea and Tea Room Talk Magazine: check out at the-leaf.org It is an e-magazine the-teaf.org/the_leaf/support-u.s.html

A Tea Reader: Katrina Avita Manichiello She has a book/anthology of tea stories and reflections. Living life one cup at a time. Tea is far more than something to quench your thirst. Tuttle Publishing.

www.stir-tea-coffee.com It is a bimonthly about the tea and coffee industry and an e-magazine.

Tea Magazine-1-800-765-2139 Check it out. You can order a copy for $5.99

Fresh Cup Magazine www.freshcup.com. It is all about coffee and tea

Tea Time-You can sign up for a newsletter at www.teamagazine.com. This is a source book for all who love tea. Very interesting with lots of photos.

The Daily Tea (used to be Tea Magazine) www.thedailytea.com. "It's not just about dry brown leaves or hot brown liquid." It is for tea lovers.

The Tea House Times-www.theteahousetimes.com. Connecting businesses and consumers since 2003 with tea publication, tea education, and more.

The Tea and Coffee Trade Journal-the monthly industry magazine.

The Leaf-a Taiwan based e-magazine dedicated to introducing the wealth of information about tea in China to English speaking audiences.

The Tea News-an online, weekly industry publication.

Imbibe-A monthly consumer oriented publication that covers a wide range of beverages including teas, cocktails, coffees and more.

Global Tea Hut-International Tea Community and a monthly mailing of a tea magazine. .

Victoria Magazine-Tea Party Bellocq Te Atelier. Bellocq is an award-winning tea company in Greenpoint, New York. Check it out online.

Here are several companies online that you can purchase tea and gifts. I know there are many more, but these are some of the ones I have used both to order tea and to write about in my novel. Check them out.

Adagio.com
Stashtea.com
Tevavana.com
Rishi-tea.com
Zhitea.com
Teaforte.com

RECIPES FOR SCONES, DRINKS, SOUPS AND ODDS AND ENDS FOR THE BONNIE NEUK TEA ROOM

SCONES

Butter is the secret to a Great Scone
Cold butter + a Hot oven = Flaky tender scones that melt in your mouth.

Lavender Blackberry Scones

3 cups flour
1/3 cup sugar
1 Tablespoon dried lavender
2 ½ teaspoons baking powder
½ teaspoon baking soda
¾ teaspoon sale
¾ cup cold butter, cut into small pats or cubes
1 large egg, lightly beaten
¾ cup cold buttermilk
1 cup fresh blackberries (fresh or frozen)
1 beaten egg and granulated sugar for sprinkle on top

Heat oven to 400 degrees.

Whisk together cream, egg and vanilla. Set aside 2 Tablespoons.

Add the rest to the dry ingredients and the chocolate chips

Mix to form a moist dough. Place dough on a floured board.

Gently pat and round it into an 8 inch circle.

Brush the dough with the reserve egg/cream mix and sprinkle with sugar.

Using a round cutter or glass, make a total of 16 scones.

Gather scraps and reshape.

Make for 20 minutes or until golden brown. Serve warm.

Scones 10-12 scones

Cranberry Pecan Scones

2/3 cup buttermilk or plain yogurt
1 egg
3 cups flour
4 teaspoons baking powder
1 /2 teaspoon baking soda
dash of salt
1 stick unsalted butter, cold and cut into 8 pieces
1 cup fresh or frozen cranberries
1/2 cup chopped pecans
1 /2 cup sugar
1 teaspoon grated orange peel (optional)
1 Tablespoon soft butter

Heat over to 375 degrees.

Measure buttermilk or yogurt in a two cup or larger glass measuring cup.

Beat in egg with a fork.

Put flour, baking powder, baking soda and salt in a large bowl.

Stir to mix.

Add 8 tablespoons butter and cut in to the flour with a pastry blender or a fork.

Add cranberries, sugar, and orange peels.

Toss lightly to distribute.

Stir buttermilk into mixture with a fork to form dough.

Turn onto a floured counter or board.

Knead 6-8 times and form into a ball.

Cut into 8 wedges and then roll each into a ball then flatten just a bit.

Place on an ungreased cookie sheet.

Bake 20-25 minutes, check for done-ness, may need 5 more minutes.

Place on a rack and brush with 1 Tablespoon of soft butter.

Serve with jellies and jam, Devonshire cream. Makes 8 scones

Chai Spiced Scones

(you can also use Earl Grey tea bags)
3 cups flour
dash of salt
¾ cup sugar
5 teaspoons baking powder
½ teaspoon cinnamon
¼ teaspoon nutmeg
¾ cup cold butter cut in pats
1 cup milk
2 tea bags Chai Tea (or Earl Grey)
2 teaspoons vanilla
Glaze:
1 cup confectioners sugar
2 teaspoons vanilla
dash of cinnamon
1-2 teaspoons milk

In a sauce pan pour 1 cup milk and heat.

Add 2 teabags of Chai (or Earl Grey) and heat to **almost** a boil.

Remove from stove and let steep for 15-20 minutes.

Add the vanilla to the milk.

Remove tea bags, making sure to squeeze all the liquid out of the tea bags.

Mix flour, salt, sugar, baking powder and spices.

Cut in cold butter pats either with a pasty blender or a fork.

Cool milk and add to the flour and butter mixture.

Combine gently.

Roll the dough on a floured board so it is round and about ½ in thick.

Cut into 8 wedges.

Place on a cookie sheet and bake at 350 degrees for 15 minutes or until golden brown.

Glaze:

Mix sugar and cinnamon together.

Add 1 Tablespoon of milk at a time and mix.

Stir until a thick paste.

Spread on the top of the hot scones.

Serve warm.

Buttermilk Blueberry Scones or Blackberry Scones

2 cups flour
6 tablespoons cold butter (cut in pieces or pats)
1/3 cup sugar
2 teaspoons baking powder
¼ teaspoon baking soda
¼ teaspoon salt
½ teaspoon vanilla
1 egg
2/3 cup buttermilk
1 cup blueberries (fresh or frozen)
Topping:
2-3 tablespoons buttermilk
1-2 teaspoons sugar

Bake at 400 degrees.

Combine flour, sugar, baking powder, baking soda and salt.

Add butter pieces to dry mix.

Mix together with a pastry cutter or fork until mixture is coarse crumbs.

Add the berries to the dry mix; coat them with dry mix.

In another bowl, combine egg, 2/3 cup buttermilk, vanilla and mix.

Create a well in the center of the dry mix.

Add buttermilk to the well.

Carefully combine until moistened.

Pour mixture on a floured board.

Spray hands with cooking spray so they don't stick and knead the dough.

You have a design choice. Either push the dough into a large circle around ½ inch thick and cut into wedges or use a drinking glass cut into shapes.

Place on baking sheet, brush with buttermilk, and sprinkle with sugar.

Bake at 400 degrees for 14-15 minutes or until golden brown.

Serves 8-10

Chocolate Chip Scones

2 ½ cups flour
½ teaspoon salt
¼ cup sugar
2 ¼ teaspoons baking powder
6 Tablespoons butter, cold, cut into pats
¾ cup cream (either half and half, light, heavy or whipping cream)
2 large eggs
2 teaspoons vanilla
1 ½ cups chocolate chips (about 9-12 oz)
Sugar for topping

Heat oven at 400 degrees.

Lightly grease a baking sheet.

Whisk together the flour, salt, sugar and baking powder.

Add butter, mixing until crumbly.

Whisk the cream, eggs and vanilla.

Set aside 2 Tablespoons and add the rest to the dry ingredients.

Add the chocolate chips. Mix to form a moist dough.

Place dough on a floured board, gently pat and round it into a 8 inch circle.

Brush dough with egg/cream mixture and sprinkle heavily with sugar.

Cut into around 12-16 round scones. using round cutter (drinking glass or cookie cutter).

Gather scraps and reshape.

Bake for 20 minutes or until golden brown. Remove and serve warm.

Plum Scones for the Red Hat Society

3 cups all purpose flour
1 /4 cup sugar
1 1 /2 Tablespoons baking powder
Dash of salt
3 /4 cup butter softened
3/4 cup buttermilk
3 eggs, beaten
1 1/2 cups pitted plums, diced

Mix together dry ingredients with electric mixer.

Add softened butter and mix by hand until crumbly.

Add butter milk and eggs.

Add diced plum and stir until moistened.

Divided batter into 3 portion and spread into 3 greased 8 inch round cake pans.

Bake at 425 degrees for 20-25 minutes.

Check center.

Cut each pan into 8 wedges.

Sour Cream Cherry Scones

2 1 /2cups all purpose flour
1 /2 cup sugar
2 teaspoon baking powder
Dash of salt
½ cup butter, softened
3 /4 cup sour cream
1 egg
1 /2 teaspoon almond extract
2/3 cup dried cherries

Topping:
1 /4 cup sliced almonds
1 Tablespoon sugar

Heat oven to 375 degrees.

Combine flour, sugar, baking powder and salt in a mixing bowl.

Mixture should be coarse crumbs.

Combine sour cream, egg and almond extract in small bowl.

Mix until smooth.

Stir in flour mixture until moist.

Stir in cherries.

Turn dough onto a lightly floured surface.

Knead 8-10 times until smooth.

You might need to add a little flour.

Divide dough in half.

Pat each half into a 7 inch circle.

Place on a greased baking sheet.

Sprinkle with topping.

Score each into 8 wedges, do not cut all the way through.

Bake 25-30 minutes until lightly brown.

Cool for 20 minutes and separate scones.

Grandma's Scottish Shortbread

1 cup unsalted butter
¾ cup confectioner's sugar
½ teaspoon vanilla or almond extract
2 ¼ cups pastry flour
¼ cup rice flour
¼ teaspoon salt

Beat butter until soft.

Add sugar and extract.

Beat until smooth.

Stir salt into flour and mix well.

Add flour mixture to butter mixture.

Press dough evenly into a round cake pan.

Score into wedges with fork.

Do not cut through the dough.

Decorate tops with fork.

Bake 375 degrees for 25 minutes, then cut along the marking while still hot.

Cool in pan.

Turn out and sprinkle with confectioner's sugar.

Serve hot or store in air tight container.

TYPES OF TEAS

Basil Tea

Basil Tea helps with intestinal colon problems, gastric ulcers, urinary infections and diarrhea. It contains iron and potassium.

Basil tea can be used in soups, over vegetables and meats or to prepare noodles or rice.

Basil with Tea

½ cup basil leaves
2 ¼ cup water
2 teaspoons tea leaves or 2 tea bags (Chai is good or use black tea)
Sugar to taste
Milk if prefer

In a small pot bring basil leaves and water to a rapid boil.

Lower the heat and allow to brew for 3-4 minutes.

Add the tea leaves or tea bag and sugar.

Again bring to a boil.

Strain into a cup.

Turmeric Ginger Tea

One of the most common uses of this herb is for its anti inflammatory properties, It detoxes the body, helps to ward off a variety of cancers, and reduces pain. Give it a try.

2 cups water
½ teaspoon powdered ginger
½ teaspoon powdered turmeric
1 Tablespoon maple syrup or honey
juice of ½ lemon

Bring water to a boil.

Reduce and add turmeric and ginger.

Simmer for 10 minutes.

Strains in a mug.

Add honey or maple syrup and lemon.

Variation:

Instead of water, use almond milk which makes a creamy turmeric tea.

Cinnamon Plum Tea (Decaf)

Black teas infused with the rich sweet flavor of plums that has been spiced with freshly ground cinnamon to create a warm, comforting cup of tea.

Blueberry Bliss Rooibos Tea (Decaf)

It is a naturally caffeine free drink with a distinctive berry taste. Low in tannin. Popular for its alleged health benefits as well as its individual flavor. Rooibos means Redbush in Afrikaans and grows only in the Cederberg mountains area of South Africa on small shrubby bushes that produce its green, needle like leaves. When fermented, the leaves turn red, making a rich-colored full bodied tea. To create Blueberry Rooibos add a mixture of blueberries, elderberry and rosehip. The result is a sweet and luscious blend that can be enjoyed at any time of day.

SMOOTHIES MADE WITH TEAS

Green Tea Smoothies

2 cups green tea, very strong. Steep for 10-15 minutes then put in an ice cube tray and freeze.
1/3 cup yogurt
½ cup Almond milk (or soy milk or any type of milk)
1 cup honey dew melon, cubed
2 Tablespoon honey (or other sugars)

Pour the strong green tea ice cubes into blender.

Add other ingredients.

Blend until smooth and serve.

Blend until smooth.

Blueberry and Banana Green Tea Smoothie

1 cup frozen blueberries
1 medium frozen banana
1 ½ cup almond milk, or any other choice of milk
1 green tea bag

Warm 1 cup of milk on stove.

Put tea bag in milk on stove and cook low for at least 5 minutes.

Put milk in freeze for a little to cool.

Pour tea/milk, ½ cup milk, frozen blueberries and frozen banana into blender and puree.

Serve cold.

Chai Tea Smoothie

¾ cup milk (soy milk, almond milk)
½ cup silken tofu (or plain yogurt)
1 Chai tea bag
1 Tablespoon sugar substitute (or use honey)
¼ teaspoon vanilla
Ice cubes
Ground cinnamon for garnish

Heat milk and put Chai tea bag in it; allow to steep for 5-10 minutes.

Add milk and remaining ingredients to the blender and puree.

Serve with cinnamon on top.

Serve cold.

Strawberry Smoothies

¾ cup strong brewed green tea
12 frozen strawberries, stems removed
1 frozen peach, pitted and cut in pieces
½ teaspoon honey
1/3 cup Greek yogurt
¼ cup milk
Ice cubes

Put all ingredients in the blender and puree.

You can also add a medium size frozen banana.

SOUPS
AT THE BONNIE NEUK

White Bean and Lime Chicken Soup

2 Tablespoons butter
1 medium yellow onion, diced
2-3 cloves garlic, minced
1 can (7 oz) green chills, chopped
1 Tablespoon cilantro, chopped
1 small Jalapeño pepper, remove veins and seeds
1 can (29 oz) can white beans (navy and/or Great Northern)
1 can (29oz) diced tomatoes
1 teaspoon oregano
1 teaspoon cumin
Dash of cinnamon
Lime juice from 1 fresh lime (use a reamer)
1 cup chicken pieces-cut in small pieces
8 cups chicken broth
Salt and pepper to taste

Saute butter, onions, garlic in a large soup pot until translucent, about 10 minutes.

Add the chopped Jalapeño pepper and green chilies and saute with other mix for 5 minutes on low heat.

Add chicken broth, tomatoes, and beans to onion mixture.

Add cilantro, oregano, cumin, cinnamon, diced tomatoes. Simmer for 30 minutes.

Add lime juice and pieces of chicken.

Heat for 5 minutes until chicken is warm.

Serve with garnish of cilantro spring. Serves 4-6

Pumpkin Soup or Pumpkin Bisque from In Addition...to the Entrée

½ cup onions chopped
3 Tablespoons butter
2 cups mashed cooked pumpkin (or canned, 20 oz can is over 3 cups)
1 teaspoon salt
1 Tablespoon sugar
¼ teaspoon nutmeg
¼ teaspoon ground pepper
3 cups chicken broth
½ cup light cream (can substitute soy milk and a little flour to thicken)

Brown onions slowly in butter.

Put mashed pumpkin into the onion pan and add salt, sugar, nutmeg and pepper. If you prefer a smooth soup, puree in food processor.

Slowly add chicken broth, mixing with wire whisk.

Heat thoroughly. Do not boil.

Slowly add the cream and reheat.

Garnish with croutons and parsley. Serves 4-5

Creamy Tomato Basil Soup

4 tomatoes, peeled, seeded and diced (or use whole tomato in can 29 oz)
4 cups tomato juice
14 leaves fresh basil
1 Tablespoon dried basil
1 cup heavy whipping cream.
¼ cup butter
Salt and pepper to taste

Simmer tomatoes, juice, basil in pot for at least 30 minutes.

Puree tomato mixture.

Put puree mixture in pot and heat on medium.

Stir in cream and butter.

Heat until melted. Do Not Boil. Serves 5-6

Lemongrass Soup with Mushrooms and Tofu

4 cups chicken stock
1 inch piece of ginger, cut into strips
3 Tablespoon lemongrass (use from a jar or fresh from an Asian market)
Thai chilies, stemmed and seeded (I start with one and increase if you like the heat)
1 Tablespoon Thai fish sauce
½ block firm silken tofu, cut into small squares
Handful of fresh shiitake mushrooms, sliced (use any type of your favorite mushroom)
1 carrot, peeled
1-2 scallion, sliced
¼ cup bamboo shoots
½ bunch fresh cilantro, chopped
Juice of 1 lime

Combine ginger, lemongrass and chilies in a medium pot.

Add the stock and fish sauce and bring to a boil.

Then reduce to a simmer and cover for about 25 minutes.

Strain all solid ingredients from stock.

Bring stock to a light boil and add mushrooms, tofu and bamboo shoots.

Let cook 10-15 minutes.

Add the lime juice.

Serve in bowls.

Garnish with ribboned carrots, scallions and cilantro.

To ribbon a carrots:

Peel carrot.

Take the peeler and holding the thickest end, peel the carrot away from you in ribbons

Tomato Basil in Soups and Stews...Comfort by the Spoonful by Connie Hope

¼ cup olive oil (or less)
2 carrots, peeled and chopped
½ large yellow onion, chopped
1-2 cloves of garlic, minced
2 Tablespoon dried basil
2 can (14.5 oz or 1 can 29 oz) tomato puree
1 can (14.5 oz) diced tomatoes
3 cups chicken broth
Salt and pepper to taste
1/4 cup fresh basil cut for garnish

Warm oil and add carrots, onion and dried basil.

Saute until tender.

Add cans of tomato puree mix. Bring to a boil.

Reduce and simmer for 10 minutes so flavor blends.

Puree soup in food processor.

Return to pot and heat.

Add salt and pepper to taste. Garnish with basil.

Serves 5-6

Cream of Asparagus Soup

2 tablespoons butter
2 tablespoons flour
1/2 teaspoon salt
1/8 teaspoon pepper
2 cups milk
3/4 pound fresh asparagus
Boiling water
salt and pepper to taste

Make the white sauce:

Melt butter in a saucepan over low heat.

Blend in flour, 1/2 teaspoon salt and 1/8 teaspoon pepper.

Stir until smooth. Add milk stirring constantly, until mixture thickens and begins to bubble. Set aside.

Wash asparagus and cut in 1/2-inch pieces.

Cook asparagus in a small amount of boiling water until tender, about 5 minutes.

Drain, reserving the cooking liquid. Set aside a few of the asparagus tips for garnish, if desired. Mash or blend remaining asparagus; set aside.

Add enough boiling water to cooking liquid to make 1 cup; add white sauce and pureed asparagus.

Heat thoroughly; season to taste with salt and pepper.

Add whole asparagus pieces and serve. Serves 4 to 6.

SALADS

Mediterranean Chickpea Salad

1-15 oz can of chickpeas (garbanzo bean) drained and rinsed
1 ½ cup cherry tomatoes, cut in half
½ red onion, chopped fine
1 cucumber, remove skin and chop
1 Tablespoon fresh parsley, chopped
1 Tablespoon fresh oregano, chopped
1/3 cup feta cheese crumbled. (also can use blue cheese)
1 Tablespoon lemon juice
1 Tablespoon extra virgin olive oil
Salt and pepper to taste

In a bowl combine the first 7 ingredients.

Add lemon juice and oil and toss to coat.

Salt and pepper to taste. Serves 8

Variation:

Substitute basil for oregano or use thyme.

Add 8 oz jar of artichoke hearts.

Broccoli Salad

2 heads fresh broccoli (just the florets)
1 medium red onion, chopped fine
6-8 strips of bacon, crispy
½ cu nuts (pecans or cashews)
½ cup dried cranberries
1 cup mayonnaise (or use ½ mayo and ½ yogurt
2 Tablespoons sugar
4 Tablespoons vinegar (I prefer rice vinegar, but you can use
your favorite)

Combine ingredients in a large bowl.

Toss to cover with sugar and vinegar.

Refrigerate for several hours before serving. Serves 8-10

SANDWICHES

Chicken Salad

2 cups chopped cooked chicken
2 Teaspoon Dijon mustard
1 cup mayonnaise (or ½ mayonnaise and ½ sour cream)
1 Tablespoon fresh lemon juice
2 cups celery, finely chopped
2 Tablespoons poppy seeds
2 cups seedless grapes (red or green)
Salt and pepper to taste
½ cup pecan (optional)

Combine all ingredients except pecan.

Stir well ; all salt and pepper to taste.

Refrigerate until ready to serve. Then add pecans and fold in.

Egg Salad

8 eggs boiled for 5 minutes, then let set in hot water for 10
Peel and chop
1 Tablespoon yellow mustard
½ cup mayonnaise
½ teaspoon fresh basil, chopped
½ teaspoon fresh parsley, chopped
¼ teaspoon garlic salt
Salt and pepper to taste
½ teaspoon onion powder
½ cup finely chopped celery

Combine all ingredients except eggs and celery.

Mix well.

Fold in the eggs and celery.

Serve on crustless bread that has been cut in quarters.

Goat Cheese and
Watercress Tea Sandwiches

2-5 ½ oz logs of soft fresh goat cheese
½ cup watercress leaves, chopped
8 soft croissants, cut in half (you can also use bread crustless,
filled and cut in quarters)
Salt and pepper to taste
½ cup pecans, chopped (optional)

Mix cheese and chopped watercress.

Salt and pepper to taste.

Spread on the ½ cut croissant.

Sprinkle small amount of chopped pecans on top (optional).

Chill before serving.

Serve with springs of watercress as garnishing.

QUICHES AND
ODDS AND ENDS

Mini Veggie Quiches

¾ cup liquid egg substitute or 3 large eggs or ¾ cup egg whites
1 package frozen chopped spinach or one fresh bunch fresh spinach
¾ cup shredded reduced fat cheese
¼ cup diced red or green or other colored peppers or mix them
¼ cup diced onions
Dash of hot pepper sauce
Salt and pepper to taste

Heat over 350 degrees.

Spray muffin tin cups with cooking spray or use paper cups. This way the quiches will not stick.

Thaw and drain spinach. Wring out so most of the liquid is removed.

Mix spinach, eggs cheese, peppers, onions, hot pepper sauce and salt and pepper in bowl.

Fill muffin tins with paper cup with mixture.

Bake at 350 degrees for 20 minutes. Test with a knife.

Remove from muffin cups and serve. Makes 12 mini quiches

Mini Quiches

2 sheets frozen puff pastry
4 eggs
¼ cup milk
½ cup mashed potatoes
½ cup mashed or pureed carrots
1 cup grated cheese

Place pastry sheets on a work surface to defrost for 10 minutes.

Preheat oven 350 degrees.

Use one 24 hole cupcake pan or 2two 12 holed cupcake pan.

Cut 12 holes in each pastry sheet with a scone cutter.

Carefully push pastry circles into pan.

Divide cheese between pastry circle and put inside.

Whisk eggs and milk together. Then whisk in mashed potatoes and carrots.

Put egg mixture into pastry cases to below the top, Bake 15 minutes or until golden. Makes 24

Devonshire Cream

1 8 ounce package cream cheese, room temperature
½ cup sour cream, room temperature
1 Tablespoon sugar

In a large bowl combine cream cheese and sour cream.

Beat well with a hand mixer until blended, smooth.

Add one teaspoon of sugar at a time and blend.

Taste to see if it is sweet enough.

Add more sugar as needed. Keep refrigerated.

Yield: about 1 ½ cup Devonshire cream.

Variation:

Instead of the ½ sour cream, use 1 cup heavy cream.

Place the cream cheese, sugar in a bowl.

Beat in cream until stiff peaks form in the bowl.

Chill until ready to serve.

Devonshire cream is also known as clotted cream. If you wanted to make the original English Clotted cream, plan on spending lots of time waiting for it. This one is a good second and the time taken is much less.

Fig and Pistachio Stuffing for Pork Loin

1 cup figs, trimmed and sliced thin
½ cup bread cubes (stuffing bread)
4 Tablespoons butter (½ stick)
¼ cup onion, chopped
1 stalk of celery, chopped
1 clove of garlic
2 teaspoons rosemary
1 cup pistachios nuts, chopped
½ cup chicken broth (if needed)
Cord soaked in water
Pork Loin

Melt butter in a frying pan.

Add onion, celery, garlic and rosemary.

Cook vegetables until soft, stirring occasionally.

Mix vegetables in bowl; add figs, bread cubes, pistachios
nuts, and a little broth.

Cut slice in the pork loin (almost all the way through)

Stuff with fig and pistachio mix.

Tie the pork loin with the soaked cord.

Cook at 350 degrees for 40-60 minutes. Test for light pink inside.

Lavender Honey

16 oz light honey
4 Tablespoon dried lavender flowers

Warm the honey in a saucepan over low heat.

Stir in lavender.

Remove from heat and let stand for about 24 hours to infuse the taste
and smells of the lavender.

Warm honey again until liquid will pour freely.

Take a wire sieve and place a coffee filter in it.

Pour liquid in the sieve and into a large glass measuring cup.

Then pour into individual small jars (or canning jars) that have lids.

Maybe a fancy bow would look good.

Refrigerate; then you can give as gifts.

Great on scones, biscuits or bread.

PHOTO OF THE ORIGINAL BONNIE NEUK TEA ROOM IN 1932

Daisy Thornall

913 Middlesex Avenue

Metuchen, New Jersey

AUTHOR'S NOTES

When one begins the task of chronologically remembering experiences by breathing life into plain words, it gives feelings to a circle of thoughts or meanings. This recalling is done with the hope that in a small way these words will create a sense of wonder and knowledge and aid in you the reader's enlightenment on your path of wonder. It was through my research into many avenues of love, spirit guides, enlightenment, and psychic ability that I began to put together this story to show you the path I took. Perhaps it will help you recognize the path to take or at least to appreciate and consider it as viable and certainly possible. It is my belief that we don't die, but leave our earthly bodies and exist on another plane. Whether it is a parallel plane or a heavenly plane is something I don't know and guess at some point I will discover. I certainly believe in heaven and that God and Jesus will be there when we die. And, as I have read, many of our loved ones will greet us at the gates of Heaven and welcome us with love and light. I don't fear death now.

We on earth can communicate with the dead. To me this is a fact. It is something I have known in my core for many years. Whether we do this via mediums, psychic assistance, spirit guides, dreams, Electronic Voice Phenomena (EVP), or many other methods, we can and do communicate with the dead. Some may not recognize this method of communication as valid and pass it off as chance or a crazy whim but, to my being, it is real. I have had it happen too many times to be just chance. I hope it happens more often; in fact; it is my desire to nurture these thoughts and leave myself open for future communications. I feel this has been the path to the creation of this book and has led me to follow through with the research for its creation. It is a path I must follow without question. May you enjoy the story, learn from its lessons, and grow from its insights. Each of us has a reason to follow our calling on earth. Mine has been to write stories that have a linear point for each of you to follow and grow from it.

Each one of you has a calling, be it earthly, spiritual, or somewhere in between. Learn from one another, from mistakes, and grow-at all times...grow.

One of the books I have used as a reference had an acknowledgement, and I quote:

"To Connie, The very first angel I met on earth, who showed me how to catch the sun." My name is Connie, and I have had visions and feelings all my life.